A BRITISH ARMY helicopter flies in low over a remote
and lonely part of the Irish border. On board are five
soldiers. Their mission, to assist Sergeant Striker. But who is
Striker? A member of their regiment, or of the SAS? And
what is his mission?

On the far side of the river, their activities are observed by
an IRA active service unit led by the Hawk who, because of
his lone and lethal campaign in the border area, has become
one of Ireland's most wanted men.

As the two pit their wits against each other, Striker is
determined both to end the career of the Hawk, and discover
the new weapon which he believes him to have. The weapon,
however, is not so readily available, even to the Hawk.

Caught in the middle of this confrontation are two
teenagers who share a deadly secret, though little else, as
they engage in a bitter conflict of their own.

In *Rainbows of the Moon,* Tom McCaughren weaves all
the elements of the Northern Ireland 'troubles' — the
conflicting loyalties, the deeply-rooted traditions of both
sides, the plight of those caught between two opposing
factions — into a story that is vividly written, utterly
compelling.

TOM McCAUGHREN, a native of Northern Ireland, is
Security Correspondent of RTE, the Irish radio and
television station, and is the author of a number of books
which have won him wide acclaim.

These include adventure stories for young people, and
a series of wildlife books which have been translated into
various languages.

His writings have earned him the Reading Association
of Ireland children's book award, the Irish Book Award for
young people's books, and selection for the prestigious
White Ravens Exhibition of the International Youth
Library in Munich.

A burst of sudden wings at dawn,
Faint voices in a dreamy noon,
Evenings of mist and murmurings,
And nights with rainbows of the moon

– FRANCIS LEDWIDGE

Tom McCaughren

RAINBOWS
of the MOON

ANVIL BOOKS

First published in hardback in 1989 by
Anvil Books Limited
45 Palmerston Road, Dublin 6.
Paperback edition 1990

4 6 8 9 7 5

ISBN 0 947962 51 4

*The characters in this novel
are imaginary and any apparent similarity
to any persons living or dead
is purely coincidental.*

Cover design Terry Myler
Typesetting Computertype Limited
Printing Colour Books Limited

For
Rena, Margaret and Dan

Chapter One

The lake was quiet, deceptively quiet, almost as if nature was aware that the forces of violence were at work.

In the shallows, edging on to a field where sheep nibbled nervously, tall green reeds with purple seed heads kept up a continuous rustle as they nodded and swayed like brittle cane in a gentle breeze.

Above them, a single swallow streaked towards the clumps of sally bushes, flipped, and with a slight flutter of its wings skimmed the dark brown waters, intent on its quest for food and impervious to the movements of either man or beast below.

Other small birds, however, had secreted themselves in the sallies and had ceased to sing.

The black-faced mountain sheep shifted about uncertainly, occasionally emitting a plaintive bleat, a mindless mass of frightened eyes and blue-dyed wool.

Farther up the lake, two swans with an entourage of four large brown cygnets moved with infinitely more grace as they glided quietly towards the more secluded upper reaches of their home.

All, except the swallow, were making way for the only other movement on the lake, a movement that was man-made.

Watched by unseen eyes, a model boat, white as a seagull and not much bigger, made its way across the lake where the water narrowed in the middle between two outcrops of rock. Now and then its whiteness sparkled in the sun, and its shadow, flitting over the muddy bottom, sent shoals of perch and other predators of the deep lunging for cover.

As the model boat passed the half-way mark, a mayfly fluttered up from the surface of the water. Slightly less white than the boat, and with a distinctive streaming tail, it had lived as a nymph on the bed of the lake for three years before floating to the surface and emerging from its nymphal case. But whatever about the miracle of its metamorphosis, it had chosen the wrong time and the wrong place to emerge. May was almost two months gone, and it was now flying in the face of both nature and man.

Behind the rocks, several crouching camouflaged figures were watching the progress of the model boat as it came towards them. Suddenly there was a shout, and the sharp crackle of rifle-fire shattered the stillness of the lake.

From the other side of the narrow neck of water another group of shadowy figures returned the fire, and in an instant a deadly hail of lead was slicing through the air where the mayfly had been.

As if deflected by the gun-fire, the model boat veered off course to take a more erratic and much less certain path down the middle of the lake.

From the cover of a rock at the lower end of the lake, other eyes now watched the boat zig-zagging towards them. For such a small craft, the lake had the dimensions of an inland sea and the slight swell the enormity of ocean waves. Its progress, therefore, seemed terribly slow, especially to the young eyes that watched and waited while at the same time sheltering from the gun-fire.

For a moment there was a lull in the shooting, and venturing to peep around the rock a little farther, the young eyes could see the gunmen lying back to reload, then rolling into position to resume their duel across the water.

The boat was now bobbing up and down as it negotiated

8

the rougher ripples of the shallower water that rolled into the lake shore. It was almost there. Another metre and two youthful hands reached out to take it.

It wasn't until that moment that each of the boys realised the other was there. So intent had they been in sheltering from the gun-fire and watching the boat that they had been completely unaware of each other's presence. It was only when they reached out from their respective sides of the rock to claim the boat that they came face to face.

Even as the gun battle raged, the two boys stopped and stared at each other. So great was their surprise, it seemed for a moment that the meeting of their eyes was frozen in time. Each had a hand on the boat; nothing was said, but their eyes told each other clearly that they were laying claim to it.

A bullet now zipped into the water beyond the boat. Casting a frightened glance at the scene of the battle, both boys hurriedly withdrew the boat from the water and, with its small plastic propellor now racing madly, lifted it up over the rock. As they did so, a hail of bullets ricocheted off the rock and whined away into the sallies.

Both boys were still holding on to the boat as they slid down behind the rock, one with a hand on the stern, the other a hand on the bow, each determined not to give up possession. Both, however, were also very frightened. They knew they were in great danger — although just how great they couldn't possibly have imagined — and somehow the high-pitched whirring of the propellor seemed to add to the urgency of the situation.

Pausing for just a split second, one of them flicked a small on-off switch which he spotted beside the tiny imitation steering-wheel, and as the propellor came to a stop they took off.

Crouching low, and each still with a hand on the boat, they ran for their lives across the short distance between the

9

lake and the sallies, hoping all the time that the rock was still shielding them from the men with the guns. As they reached the sallies, they could hear more bullets whistling through the upper branches. Not even pausing to look back, they scrambled over a strand of barbed wire and pushed their way in under the bushes.

Oblivious of the squelching mud and scratching undergrowth, they continued to claw their way forward, spurred on by a common desire to get as far away from the shooting as possible, and held together by the boat, to which they both clung with the greatest tenacity.

Not until they had left the scrubland well behind, and concealed themselves in a small copse of birch trees from which they could see the lake, did the two boys pause to get their breath and take stock of the situation.

'They were shooting as us there,' panted one of them. 'Bloody Brits.'

'Bloody IRA,' retorted the other.

Ignoring each other's remark for the moment, they looked down at the lake. The shooting was now more sporadic than before, and they could see that the two groups were disengaging, with the back-markers exchanging parting shots to cover their retreat to the woods. The group on the left were clearly members of a British army patrol. The others were civilians, and judging by the way one was being helped along they had suffered a casualty.

One of the boys sat down, pulling the boat with him. Taking stock of the other boy, who was now forced to sit down too, he could see he was freckled-faced and sandy-haired. He was also taller, and wore an army combat jacket, trousers and boots. 'I thought you were a bloody Brit for a minute,' he told him. 'Wearing gear like that.'

The taller boy looked at his equally unwelcome companion who was wearing a light, blue and green jacket, open-necked shirt and jeans. 'It's as good as yours. Anyway, is that all you can do, swear?'

'Well, you swore a minute ago. You said, "The bloody IRA".'

'You provoked me. In any case, that's what they are.'

'Are what?' asked the smaller boy.

'Bloody killers.'

'It's the British army that are the killers.'

The taller boy snorted and turned his head away. However, he still held on to the boat.

'The boat's mine,' said the smaller boy. 'I saw it first.'

The other boy turned to face him. 'That's a lie. Furthermore, I got my hand to it first, and that's what matters.'

'You did not,' said the smaller boy, jerking the boat towards him.

'I did so,' said the other, jerking it back.

As they stared at each other, the taller boy could see that his opponent — for that is what he now considered him to be — had wavy black hair and black eyebrows, and had reached the stage where he was getting spots on his face. It was a problem he himself didn't have yet, but he reckoned they were about the same age. 'Who are you anyway?' he asked.

'My name's James.'

'What's your second name?'

'James Pius.'

'You're a papish!'

'And what if I am?'

'I might have known it,' said the taller boy. 'I meant what was your second name? Your surname?'

'It's none of your business. I don't even know your first name.'

'If it's any of your business, my name's William.'

James Pius turned his head away, saying, 'A Prod. A black Prod,' and spat on the grass to emphasise his disgust.

Both boys now lapsed into silence to brood upon their misfortune in having met up with each other, and to think how they were going to get sole possession of the boat.

James Pius had never met a Protestant before. The phrase 'black Protestant' kept going through his mind as he tried to grapple with the situation, and he couldn't help stealing a glance at this one who had the affrontery to lay claim to his boat. Just what was meant by a 'black Protestant' he didn't really know. This one didn't look any blacker than anyone else; not even as black as himself. No, he thought, it was something else that was meant. Probably something to do with their religion or customs. Some of them, he had been told, had very peculiar customs. In his view they were also the people with the money, the good land, the good jobs, the big cars. Well, he thought, there was no way they were going to get their hands on the boat too. That was his, and nobody was going to take it away from him.

For his part, William was wondering how he had come to be shackled to what he called a 'papish'. It had always been a case of 'them' and 'us', he thought, the two communities living separately, each suspicious of the other. The churches to which 'they' went and the frequency of their church-going had always been a mystery to him; their games distant and foreign. It was a gap which had widened as the IRA's campaign of violence had intensified. And here he was, sitting beside one of 'them' now, even talking to him. 'Well, if he thinks he's going to get the boat,' said William to himself, 'he's got another think coming.'

It was only now as the two turned to focus their attention on the object of their thoughts that they took their first really good look at the boat. It was a cabin cruiser, about 18 inches long, and modelled to perfection. There were silvery rails around the deck, small make-believe windows on the sides of the cabin, and even a short aerial on the front right-hand corner of the cabin for a radio. In fact, it was complete in every detail, right down to the small flag on the stern.

'Green, white and gold!' exclaimed William. 'That's the Free State flag!'

'What about it?' asked James Pius defiantly.

'There'll be no foreign emblems on my boat.'

'Foreign emblems? That's the Tricolour, man, and anyway, you should be proud of it. That's not gold, it's orange — for the Protestants of the North.'

'For the Protestants? Huh! That's a good one. That's the Free State flag; it represents everything that's foreign to us and I'm not going to have it on my boat.'

'I told you before, it's not your boat.'

There was another hostile silence.

'Maybe,' said William after a while, 'it doesn't belong to either of us.'

'It was out of control,' James Pius reminded him. 'Abandoned.'

William thought for a moment. 'Maybe the real owner was down there among the rocks, taking shelter from the bullets, just the way we were.'

'If the Brits haven't shot him.'

'Or the IRA.'

'How could the IRA have shot him?' asked James Pius. 'Sure he must have been on the same side of the lake as they were. The boat was coming from the South. And look at the name of it— *Erin go Bragh*.'

The name was painted on the stern in small gold lettering, and William hadn't seen it before as he was holding the bow. 'What does it mean?'

'Ireland For Ever.'

'Well, that's another thing that'll have to go,' William declared. 'There'll be no Gaelic on my boat.'

'I thought you said it might not be your boat? That the real owner might be hiding down there among the rocks?'

'Well, if the British army have shot him as you say, he'll have no need for it, will he?'

13

'Maybe,' said James Pius, 'he's wounded. Did you ever think of that?'

In fact, William hadn't thought of that possibility. 'You know, you could be right. Maybe we'd better go down and see — unless, of course, you're scared.'

'Scared? Why should I be scared? Anyway, it seems to be all over now. The Brits have run off with their tails between their legs as usual.'

'It seems to me,' said William, 'that it was the IRA who came off worst.'

James Pius got up, forcing his companion to do likewise. 'This is stupid,' he said, tugging the boat. 'I'll carry it.'

William held on.

'Only down as far as the lake. If we don't find the owner, then we can decide what we're going to do with it.'

William still held on.

James Pius jerked the boat from him. 'I'm not going to run away with it.'

'All right,' said William reluctantly. 'But only as far as the lake — and I'll be right beside you.'

Over an hour had elapsed since the gun battle, and the lake was tranquil once more.

'What do you think?' asked William as they scanned it from the cover of the sally bushes.

'Seems quiet enough.'

'Too quiet maybe. Listen.'

'I am listening,' replied James Pius. 'I can't hear a thing, except for the rustle of the reeds.'

'That's what I mean. The birds aren't singing.'

James Pius rested the cabin cruiser on the marshy ground and sighed. 'It's no wonder they aren't singing. Sure all that shooting must have frightened off every bird within ten miles of here.'

'Maybe so . . . but I still don't like it.'

James Pius lifted the boat. 'Well, you can stay here if you

like. I'm going on up the lake.'

William stepped forward, put his hand on the boat, and looked James Pius straight in the eye. 'Not without me you're not.'

James Pius shrugged. 'Suit yourself.'

Emerging from the sallies, the two of them headed up along the lake shore. As they walked, they looked anxiously around for any sign of further trouble. However, nothing untoward disturbed the stillness. The black-faced mountain sheep, frightened by the gun-fire, were still huddled in a tight flock in a corner of the field, and the only movement on the lake itself was the swallow, which had resumed its search for insects just above the surface of the water.

'There's where the IRA were firing from,' said James Pius. He put down the boat and started collecting some of the empty brass cartridge shells that had been ejected from the rifles. Not to be outdone, William also began to pick them up. The shells were scattered for a good distance along the rocky shore, testifying to the fact that the gunmen had continually changed position in an effort to confuse the soldiers and make themselves a less predictable target.

'Here's the control box,' said James Pius. 'Whoever was using it must have scarpered when the shooting began.'

'More likely the IRA used him as a shield to get away,' said William. 'They're good at that sort of thing, especially when they're armed and the other people aren't.'

'I didn't see them taking any hostage with them,' James Pius retorted. 'Only the man who was injured.'

'Maybe he was the owner of the boat. Maybe he got caught up in the gun battle.'

James Pius, who was studying a blood-stain behind one of the rocks, nodded. 'It might have been him all right.' He straightened up and looked around. 'If it was, he won't be having much use for it now.'

Seeing James Pius with the control box, William had taken

the opportunity to pick up the boat. Now, he thought, they were even.

They looked each other in the eyes again, hostile, distrusting, but before they could speak there was a burst of gun-fire, and a hail of bullets went whizzing over their heads.

Throwing a startled glance up towards the woods where the IRA men had gone, they saw flashes of gun-fire coming from the darkness between the trees. At the same time, they heard the answering crack of rifles from across the lake, and once more the air was filled with the whine of bullets.

'Come on,' cried James Pius. 'Let's get out of here. This battle isn't over yet, and we're smack in the middle of it.'

Chapter Two

Out of the corner of his left eye, Private Smith saw the two boys sprinting away along the far shore of the lake. He closed that eye and with the other squinted through the optic sight of his new Enfield rifle, the short barrel of which rested on the two legs of a bipod. Known as a times-four optical sight, because it increased the image by four, it enabled him to scan the woods where the latest volley of shots had come from. 'I can't see anything, Sarge.'

Striker adjusted his field-glasses, and grunted, 'No, but they're still there.' Like the rest of his patrol, he was lying flat on his stomach behind a small ridge of stones that were covered with ferns and moss.

'How can you be sure it's that PIRA unit, Sarge, not INLA?' The voice came from nearby, pronouncing the abbreviations for the Provisional Irish Republican Army and the Irish National Liberation Army as words rather than letters.

Striker was still looking through his binoculars intently. 'Who's that?'

'Corporal Willoughby.'

'Keep your stupid head down, Willoughby. I don't want that radio shot to pieces.'

Willoughby flattened himself even further and slid back down the stones to make sure he couldn't be seen.

'I told you who it was,' Striker added. 'Now notify base and tell them we've got contact again.'

Willoughby wasn't amused that a radio should be held to be more valuable than his own head, but then as he prepared to make his call, he had to admit Striker was right. If they found themselves in a tight corner and needed reinforcements, or indeed any kind of assistance, the radio was their only link with base. So vital was the link, in fact, that normally two of them would have radios — the patrol leader and one other — in case one of them got shot. But then, this was no normal patrol; Striker seemed to be a law unto himself.

'It's nice to know you're needed,' Willoughby thought as he whispered, 'Alpha 39 to base ...' Then, a moment later, to Striker, 'The OC still thinks you should accept reinforcements.'

'Negative,' Striker replied. He still had his binoculars trained on the woods, searching for any further sign of the active service unit.

Willoughby passed on the message and to his surprise received the reply, 'Roger. Over and out.' He was wondering, just as the other members of the patrol were wondering, how a sergeant was able to tell the commanding officer what he did or did not want.

None of them had met Striker before. He had already been operating in the area on his own, and had asked for five men to be flown in to join him. Willoughby was one; the others were Smith, Brown, Peacock and Mannering. Apart from the fact that Smith was a crack shot, there was nothing to distinguish them from any other members of their regiment; they all just happened to be resting and available when the call came.

'You, you and you!' — that's the way they were chosen. All volunteers, of course, thought Willoughby wryly. Then, he recalled, it was up and back into combat kits. Probably, they reckoned, another vehicle checkpoint, or VCP as it was known in military jargon. VCP's were easy, just so long as

18

someone was watching your back. Check drivers. Check the computer. Check the boot. Drivers sullen, hostile, unco-operative. No matter. No guns, no threat. A short stint, and it was back to the helicopter and the relative safety of the base. But not this time. This time it was blackened badges, back-packs and 24-hour rations; that meant they were staying out overnight, and that was most unusual. Most unusual indeed.

'Rendezvous with Sergeant Striker,' they were told.

'Who's Striker?'

'You'll find out. Now move it. And don't forget your cam cream. We don't want PIRA getting a look at those lily-white faces, now do we?'

'No way. But who's this Sergeant Striker?'

'You'll find out.'

A quick squeeze of camouflage cream into the palm of the hand. Light green at one end, dark green at the other. Dip in the fingers and spread it down the face. Always down, of course, to break the outline of the face; never across.

'Come on, come on, move it. And make sure those cap badges are properly blackened. We don't want to give some trigger-happy Paddy a good aiming mark. Your mother wouldn't like that, would she?'

No reply.

'Would she, Willoughby?'

'No, Sir!'

A last rub, a quick check, on with the back-packs, and then it was out and running, crouching under the rotor blades of the waiting Lynx and they were away.

'Thank God for a machine that can fly low and fast,' they thought, as they watched the pointed shadow of the helicopter speeding across the hilly terrain beneath them. 'Low and fast,' they kept saying to themselves. 'That's it; low and fast.' Too fast, hopefully, for the heavy machine-guns the IRA had got from Libya. Too low for the surface-to-

19

air missiles Colonel Gadafy was said to have given them.

The noise of the engine, the rush of the wind in the open doors. Too noisy to talk. Only time to think. The pointed shadow framed in the open doorway, still racing ahead ... almost as if it wanted to get there first ... flitting across a terrain that was forever hostile. At least, they thought, they hadn't been posted to Crossmaglen. Anywhere but Crossmaglen. Still, the whole border was dangerous, and the countryside even more dangerous than the towns and villages. One careless step, one wrong move, that's all it needed. A quiet wood, a gap in a hedge, the trip-wire of a booby-trap bomb waiting for the unwary. There were woods in the area they were going to now, they were told. And lakes. At least there would be no booby-trap bombs on the lakes. But what was their mission? No time for questions. Sergeant Striker would tell them anything else they had to know.

'Who's Sergeant Striker?'

Sweeping in low over fields that were rushy and rugged and typical of that part of the Irish border, the Lynx hovered momentarily behind a small hill. Everybody out. Rifle at the ready, head down, spongy field. The Lynx was away and they were on their own, sprinting for cover.

'Where's Striker?'

'Here he is.' And suddenly they found themselves in the bushes beside him.

Striker was tall, over six foot they reckoned, a powerful figure with a full commando pack on his back, rifle in hand and a 9 mm Browning pistol on his belt. He had been living rough; the stubble on his cream-striped face testified to that. He had the same badge on his beret as they had, blackened so as not to reflect any light, but, as they were soon to discover, apart from that he was wearing no other insignia to indicate either regiment or rank.

Their first briefing took place as they knelt in the cover of nearby woods. Striker told them he had been keeping an active service unit of PIRA under surveillance and was now planning to set up an ambush at the first opportunity.

'Where's the border?' Mannering wanted to know.

'There's a string of lakes just south of here, and it runs right through the middle of them.'

They all nodded. That figured. This border between Northern Ireland and the Republic was something else. They had soon come to learn that it ran across farms, through houses, between the parapets of bridges ... and now, believe it or not, along the middle of lakes. How were they supposed to patrol a border like that?

Striker briefed them on the terrain and the strength of resistance they might expect when they made contact.

'How many?' asked Smith.

'Three, possibly four,' he told them. But he didn't tell them everything. If he had, they might have been better prepared.

How Striker had come to know that the IRA active service unit would turn up on the other side of the lake, they couldn't imagine. But he had the patrol well concealed and lying in wait behind the rocks before there was any move on the far side of the water. Then some fool chose that very moment to start up his model boat and send it out into the middle of the lake. They had all watched it ... peering through their optic sights at the far shore with one eye, opening the other occasionally to look at the small craft's progress across the lake.

It was only when the boat continued to head straight for them that Striker raised the alarm.

'Look out!' he shouted, and opened fire.

At first they fired at the boat. 'Not the boat,' he commanded. 'Over there, behind the rocks.'

Even as they redirected their fire, they received a hail of bullets in return.

As for the boat, it had veered off to their right and they

forgot all about it until the shooting died down. Then Striker did a most unusual thing. Seeing two boys picking it out of the water at the lower end of the lake, he loosed off a burst of shots in their direction, and when they ran towards the sallies, he fired another burst.

'What did you do that for, Sarge?' asked Willoughby.

'Never mind. Just keep your head down.' He was peering through his binoculars at the far shore now. 'They're pulling back. I think we winged one of them. Okay, back up into the woods.' He fired a final burst in the direction of the far shore, and covered the others as they ran crouching from the lakeside.

Having taken up a new vantage point, the patrol reloaded their weapons and waited.

'What's this all about, Sarge?' asked Private Peacock. 'Why did you shoot at the boys?'

'I wasn't shooting *at* them. I was just trying to scare them off.'

'You did that all right,' said Smith, who had propped his rifle up on its bipod again and was peering through the optic sight at the far shore.

Mannering took off his glasses and cleaned them. 'How did you know there was a PIRA unit over there, Sarge?'

'The same way they knew we were over here.'

'How's that?' asked Brown.

'We've been playing cat and mouse for over a week,' Striker replied. He took up his field-glasses and put them to his eyes. 'Maybe we're getting to know each other too well.'

'We?' said Willoughby. 'Who is it over there — someone you know?'

Striker lowered his glasses and, gazing pensively across the lake, nodded. 'An Showick,' he said, giving a fairly accurate pronunciation of the Irish *An Seabhac*.

'An what, Sarge?'

22

'*An Seabhac* — the Hawk.'

'The Hawk!' They looked at him and he could see shock and surprise written all over their faces.

'Keep your heads down,' he warned them. 'Unless you want them blown off.'

They pressed themselves closer to the ground and peered through the optic sights of their rifles with a new respect for the enemy across the lake.

'Don't let his reputation bother you,' said Striker. 'He's no different from any of the other PIRA scum. Hit and run, that's all they're good for.'

Maybe so, they thought, but the Hawk was a name they had come to fear. They had read about him long before they had come to the North. THE HAWK STRIKES AGAIN! the tabloids back home were for ever screaming. He was hardly ever out of their headlines. THE HAWK. It was a nice four-letter word. Just right for the tabloids. THE HAWK SWOOPS. That was another favourite one. And there were many others, each recounting acts that were more bloody than the one before. HAWK PREYS ON LONE UDR MEN. HAWK ATROCITY. HAWK OUTRAGE. BLOODY HAWK. THE KILLER HAWK. Then it was the catch-cry, GET THE HAWK, with editorials demanding, FIND THIS MAN or STOP THIS ANIMAL. There were even calls on the Government to close the border. The Unionist politicians went over hotfoot to 10 Downing Street, insisting that the SAS be sent in, and then it was promises of action from the Prime Minister and the Northern Secretary. WE'LL CLIP HIS WINGS, SAYS MAGGIE, proclaimed the tabloids jubilantly. More troops were flown to the North, the problem was discussed at the Anglo-Irish Conference, and the Dublin Government promised full co-operation. However the Hawk continued to fly in the face of them all. He continued to prey upon the off-duty, the unarmed, the vulnerable and the unsuspecting. They still found his name on pieces of shrapnel

23

after he lobbed his home-made mortars into RUC stations and army barracks close to the border. They still found his victims, members of the security forces or people associated with them, lying in quiet border roads, ambushed or blown up.

And now Striker was saying, 'Don't let his reputation bother you.' He must be joking, they thought. Then they wondered, what else had he not told them?

'Why don't we alert the security forces on the other side of the border?' asked Mannering. 'And call up our own reinforcements?'

'We'd just be wasting our time,' Striker replied 'He'd dump his guns and melt into the countryside.'

Smith was lining up the top of the black arrow in his optic sight with an imaginary target on the edge of the far woods. Ironically, the arrow resembled an Irish round tower. 'I think I could nearly pick them off from here.'

'We want to be certain,' said Striker 'We'll redeploy again on the lake shore.'

'It would have been simpler to stay where we were,' Smith thought. But then he knew it was safer to change position, keep the enemy guessing.

Leaving their back-packs in the woods, they crawled through the undergrowth until they were behind a solid mound of stones on another part of the lake shore.

'What makes you think he'll be back?' asked Mannering.

'Because he may think we've withdrawn.' Striker trained his binoculars on the lower end of the lake. 'And because the boys are coming back. If I'm not mistaken, they've got something he wants.'

Through the grass and ferns that grew on top of the mound of stones, they could see the two boys climbing over a strand of barbed wire at the end of the sallies.

'You mean the boat?' asked Willoughby.

'Correct.'

'But what would he want with the boat, Sarge?' asked Smith.

Striker watched the two boys as they walked cautiously up along the far shore. 'Our intelligence indicated that the Hawk might be trying out something new. Just what it was, I didn't know — until I saw that boat coming towards us.'

'But it was only a model boat,' said Private Peacock from his left.

Striker was watching the boys picking up the empty cartridges. 'That's it. They have it now. They have the control box.'

'Control box for what?' asked Mannering.

'For the boat of course. The Hawk was sending it straight over to us.'

'But why, Sarge?'

'That's a good question, Private Brown. He must have had a surprise in it for us, wouldn't you say? And I want to find out what it is.'

Suddenly there was a volley of shots from the far woods, and they saw the two boys taking to their heels.

Striker fired a burst of shots in the general direction of the woods, saying, 'Stay where you are, Hawk. I was right. You want that boat just as badly as I do.'

Smith held his fire as he hadn't spotted a clear target. 'How come, Sarge? What's in the boat?'

'Something new, Smith. At a guess I'd say something new in the line of explosives.'

'You mean a bomb?'

Striker nodded. 'Exactly. And those two boys have just run off with it.'

Chapter Three

William and James Pius had run and run until they could run no more. Exhausted, they put down the boat and its control box and flopped on the ground beside them.

'I wonder what's going on back there?' panted William when he had got enough breath back to speak. 'I thought for a minute they were firing at us.'

James Pius took off his runners which had got muddy and wet beneath the sallies. 'The Brits aren't fussy who they fire at. When the shooting starts they just let go at anything that moves.'

'But that was the IRA that opened fire. Right over our heads.'

'Aye. But who fired at us the first time? Down at the far end of the lake? It was the Brits!'

'They were probably just warning shots,' said William.

James Pius grunted. 'Huh! Some warning.'

Lying back, they lapsed into silence as they waited for their breathing to return to normal.

After a few minutes, William sat up and looking back at the wooded hills, said, 'Did you ever get the feeling someone was watching you?'

James Pius sat up too. 'Who?'

'I don't know. You don't suppose they followed us, do you?'

'You mean, the Brits?'

'Any of them.'

'Why should any of them come after us?'

William shrugged. 'I don't know, but I've a funny feeling somebody's watching us.'

James Pius glanced back up at the woods and wondered. If anyone was watching them, it was probably the Brits, he thought. They were always spying on people, watching them from their spotter planes, their helicopters, their look-out towers and their concrete shelters. He looked at William's combat clothes and thought once again how it reminded him of the Brits. How he and his family hated that uniform — all uniforms. As Republicans, they had been watched by the security forces more than most — as they discovered to their cost.

William, however, was thinking that if anyone was watching them it was the IRA. Taking his eyes away from the woods, he picked up the model boat and looked at the name again. *Erin go Bragh*. Ireland For Ever. And he looked at the Tricolour. How he detested that flag. Somehow it seemed to symbolise the IRA. It was the flag they carried in procession; the flag in which they wrapped their dead. He had heard what James Pius had said about 'the Brits', but the British army held no fear for him or his family. It was the IRA that posed the threat to them on their isolated border farm. It was the IRA they felt were always watching them, and they were right . . .

From a small circle of boulders on the summit of a nearby hill, Sean the Hawk watched the two boys through a pair of field-glasses. 'Tell me again, Professor,' he said. 'What do you think? Is it likely to go off?'

'All depends.'

'Depends on what?'

'On how they handle it. What levers they pull, what switches they flick. Whether the control arm touches the micro-switch. It depends on a lot of things, but one way or

27

another they're only a hair's breadth away from kingdom come.'

The Hawk looked at him and his cold blue eyes seemed to bore right through him. 'If they are, so are you.' He trained his binoculars on the two boys again. 'That's Ned's son down there?'

'Who's the other one?' asked the Professor.

The Hawk spat to the side, and still looking through the glasses, replied, 'I don't know. It's Ned's son I'm worried about.' He paused. 'As for the boat ... if the Brits get their hands on it, you won't have to worry about them shooting you. I'll do it myself.' Turning around to emphasise the point, he added, 'And I won't make the same mistake they did. I won't miss.'

The Professor didn't reply to the threat. Instead he sat down, adjusted his rimless glasses so that they sat more comfortably on the bridge of his nose, and tucked in the loose end of a blood-stained bandage on his left hand.

The man the other members of the IRA active service unit called the Professor wasn't yet thirty but his tousled grey hair and his quiet, studious manner made him look older. While he hadn't responded to the threat that had just been made to him, he found it very disturbing. It wasn't only the fact that Sean the Hawk was quite capable of carrying out the threat; it was the unthinking manner in which it had been made. Here he was, one of the organisation's most valuable officers, and to think that the Hawk had even considered for one moment that he could be wasted.

As he pondered on the problem, the Professor thought that it seemed a lifetime since he had been recruited to the cause. Francey was the name by which he was known in those days. Born and reared in the middle-class suburbs of south Dublin, he hadn't given much thought to what was happening in the North.

He had been too busy studying, too busy worrying about

whether or not he would be able to get a job at home or have to take the boat to England. Perhaps it was thoughts like that that drew him into Sinn Fein. If all else failed, England would be the saviour, the place with the jobs; but then Sinn Fein speakers had presented a different view of the problem. England was responsible for Ireland's political and economic ills, they said. Always had been, always would be. Nothing would change until she was forced out of the North, and a new order established in the island as a whole.

He had moved up the educational ladder at that stage and was studying electronics. He had also involved himself in various meetings and debates. It was, after all, a time of debate, a time of free thinking. But it was also a time of opportunity, many people said. A time to do something — a time, someone suggested, to turn his talents to more practical use .

That was how he had begun to work for the IRA. However, his extracurricular activities soon came to the notice of the Special Branch. Somehow they discovered he was making circuit boards for bombs, and almost before he knew it he had graduated to another institution — the high security prison at Portlaoise.

When, eventually, he emerged from the large grey gates of the prison, he found that his talents were in even greater demand. He was older and greyer then, but it was back to school, only this time his courses of instruction were in remote mountain glens and secluded woods. There, others filled in the gaps in his education, and before long he was known in the movement not as Francey but as the Professor, and not as a student but as one of the IRA's leading experts on how to make bombs.

'How's the hand, Professor?'

He turned his head to see young Cathal sitting beside him. 'It'll be all right, Cathal Óg. Just a graze.'

Cathal Óg was leaning back against the rocks, holding his

Kalashnikov rifle between his upturned knees. 'And how about the leg?'

'Smarting a bit, but just skinned, like the hand.'

'Twice lucky,' said Seamus, the fourth member of the unit, who had come over to join them.

The Professor nodded. He reckoned a bullet had splintered on the rocks and hit him on the hand and the calf of his right leg at the same time. It had caused him to drop the control box and taken the leg from under him. Thinking he was seriously wounded, the others had helped him to hobble away from the lake and out of range.

'Why is this bomb in the boat so important?' asked Cathal Óg.

The Professor leaned his head back against the rocks and thought for a moment.

'In simple language,' said Seamus, and Cathal Óg nodded. They sometimes found the Professor's explanations tedious and difficult to understand.

'Well,' the Professor told them, 'in simple language we ... have been experimenting and have succeeded in making our own type of plastic explosive.'

'But why?' asked Cathal Óg. 'Didn't we get loads of Semtex from Libya?'

The Professor nodded. 'True, and we would have got another shipload of it if the French hadn't seized the *Eksund* in 1987.' He paused for a moment before continuing. 'Semtex, as you know, is made in Czechoslovakia. It's the most powerful plastic explosive available, and it's been a great boost to our campaign.'

Seamus interrupted him. He had been introduced to Semtex on one of his training courses, but had been afraid to show his ignorance by asking why it was called a plastic explosive. He thought it was because it was like putty or plasticine, but he wasn't sure.

'You're right,' said the Professor. 'Anything that can be

30

shaped or moulded is a plastic. Semtex is also light and easily transportable.'

'Why do we want to try and make our own then?' asked Cathal Óg.

'Well, we have to plan ahead. We never know when the guards or the Brits might stumble across our supplies.'

Seamus gripped his Kalashnikov. 'Or when they might force somebody into informing.'

'Exactly,' said the Professor. 'And we don't know how long our campaign is going to take. So we've been experimenting.'

'You mean we've succeeded in making our own Semtex?' asked Cathal Óg.

The Professor nodded. 'More or less. What we've made is our own version of RDX. That's what the armies in this part of the world use, including the Brits. It's one of the ingredients of Semtex, and is practically the same.'

'And is RDX also a plastic explosive?' asked Seamus.

'It's a powder you get from boiling three chemicals. You make it into a plastic explosive by mixing it with oil and chalk. That allows you to shape it whatever way you want.'

'Why would you want to shape it?' asked Cathal Óg.

'Because it means you can do anything you want with it. You can roll it into a ball, stick on to the lock of a door, even make it as thin as a slice of cheese. But the point is that, by moulding it in certain ways, you can make it more powerful.'

'How come?' asked Cathal Óg.

'Well, you can enhance the effect by shaping the charge in such a way that the force of the blast goes in a particular direction.'

'So you were trying out a shaped charge of your new explosive in the *Erin go Bragh?*' said Cathal Óg.

The Professor nodded. 'We're also anxious to get that guy in charge of the patrol. He's been bugging us for a while now.'

'But we don't want him to get the boat, do we, Professor?' Sean the Hawk had come back to join them. 'Our intelligence says he's an SAS man called Striker, and we don't want him to find out what we're doing, do we?' There was silence for a moment. 'The idea was to blow *him* to kingdom come — not to hand him our secrets on a plate, or should I say, on a boat. Isn't that right, Professor?'

'But he didn't get the boat,' said Seamus. 'Anyway, how could he know what's in it?'

The Hawk looked at him. 'The Brits have their ways. If he didn't want the boat, why did he stop firing at it and start firing at us?'

'But he doesn't have the boat,' said the Professor. 'The boys have it.'

'And all we have to do is tell them it's ours,' said Seamus.

'If it doesn't blow up before we get the chance,' said the Hawk.

'What if it does?' asked Seamus. 'The Brits wouldn't know what was in it, would they?'

'Maybe not, but as I told you before, one of those boys is Ned's. He's the only son he has at home now, and if he goes up with it we're all in trouble.' The Hawk looked hard at the Professor. 'Tell me again, Professor, how likely is it to go off when they handle it?'

The Professor pushed his glasses back up from the bridge of his nose and fiddled with the bandage on his injured hand. He had constructed the *Erin go Bragh* with great care and was very proud of it. Using a small amount of RDX, he had made a curve-shaped bomb and fitted it into the cabin, the idea being, as he had explained to the others, to direct the shrapnel forward in a more lethal arc.

'I know the principle of it,' said the Hawk impatiently. 'But how likely is it to go off? And why didn't it go off when we wanted it to?'

'Well,' said the Professor, 'you know the control box has

two fairly big levers, or joysticks as they're called. The one on the right is for direction. The other one is to set off the bomb.'

'So if they monkey around with the second one, they could blow themselves up?' asked the Hawk.

'Maybe, maybe not. It's not that simple.'

Sean the Hawk swore quietly to himself. Nothing was ever simple with people like the Professor. He knew he must try to be patient if he was to get a straight answer. 'Will you try to explain it, as simply as you can?'

'Well, behind each joystick is a smaller lever. When the small lever on the right is in the centre, the boat will set off in a straight line, and then you can use the joystick to direct it any way you want.'

'And when the one behind the other joystick is in the centre,' asked the Hawk, 'what happens?'

'Then that joystick can set off the bomb.'

'How does it do that?' asked Seamus.

'There's a control arm inside the boat. It's made of white plastic and is shaped like a starfish. The joystick causes that to move so that it makes contact with the micro-switch and sets off the bomb.'

'And why didn't it go off for you?' asked the Hawk.

The Professor lowered his eyes. He couldn't admit that at the last moment he had discovered he had failed to set the small lever on the left in the correct position, so he said. 'The shot made me drop the control box and then the boat veered off course.'

The Hawk's eyes narrowed. He suspected that somehow the Professor had been at fault, but he couldn't be sure. 'So if they mess around with the levers and switches it could go off?'

The Professor nodded. 'The small wooden plug I inserted in the stern of the boat, just above the water-line — that was a safety device. It ensured that the bomb didn't go off prematurely or accidentally. But you'll remember that as the boat moved off I pulled out the plug with the fishing-line.'

The Hawk nodded.

'When that was pulled out, the circuit was completed and the bomb was ready to operate.'

'And if the levers aren't in the proper position,' asked the Hawk, 'how safe is it?'

The Professor shrugged. 'The whole thing is very sensitive. Messing around with the control box or the switches, even messing with the boat itself, will set the starfish flicking back and forth, and then it's touch and go whether it depresses the micro-switch far enough to make contact.'

The Hawk sighed. 'Right then. You'd better get down there fast and get it back before it goes off. We'll give you cover.'

As they got up to go, a single shot rang out and a bullet ricocheted off the rocks in front of them.

'Down!' cried the Hawk, and as they dived for cover he gritted, 'Damn you, Striker. You're still out there, and I was right. You *are* after the boat.'

Chapter Four

Before the shot rang out, James Pius and William had been discussing the boat.

'What are we going to do with it?' asked William.

'Do with it? We're going to keep it. Or at least I am.'

William scowled at him. 'If that's what you think, you've another think coming. Anyway, what I mean is, afterwards, after we've finished with it. How are we going to get it back to the man who owns it?'

James Pius shook his head. 'Forget it. Whoever had it on the lake has been shot. There's no way he's going to go back there looking for it, and I can tell you one thing for sure, there's no way I'm going back there.'

William was silent. While he wanted the boat for himself, he knew it belonged to someone else. Yet James Pius was right. They couldn't go back to the lake again; it would be suicidal to do so. At the same time, there was no way he was going to hand over ownership, however temporary it might be, to James Pius.

Picking up the boat he looked again at the name on the stern. 'I wonder what the hole is for?'

'Where?'

'Here. Just above the water-line?'

James Pius took the boat, closed one eye and put the other close to the hole. He couldn't see inside, but as he looked at the hole his eyes fell on the small on-off switch beside the imitation wheel on the wall of the cabin beyond. 'This

35

is the one that switched it off,' he said, and as he flicked it on, the small plastic propeller immediately whirred into life.

'Turn it off,' said William. 'You'll run down the battery.'

As James Pius did so, his fingers found a second switch in under the cabin roof, but it didn't seem to do anything.

'And there's another one here on the control box,' said William. 'It's still on ...' He flicked it back and forth and each time it was at the 'on' position he could see a silvery needle moving up past red to green on a small dial in front of it. Apart from that, however, it didn't seem to do anything either.

James Pius shook his head. 'I don't know. We'll try it out at the next lake we come to.'

On the hill above, the Professor had watched them. He knew that as they worked at the various switches and controls the white plastic starfish he had described to the others was jerking and trembling inside the boat, and that one arm of it was flicking dangerously close to the micro-switch that would detonate the bomb. As he had told the Hawk, they were at that moment within a hair's breadth of being blown to kingdom come.

The boys, however, were blissfully unaware of the lethal nature of what they held in their hands.

'Where were you going anyway?' asked James Pius. 'When you stopped at the lake?'

William didn't answer right away. Then he said, 'Hiking. What about you?'

'To my grandfather's. I'm going to spend the weekend with him.' James Pius was now pushing the switch on the control box on and off, and as he watched the silvery needle flicking up past red to green said, 'I think that means the battery's okay.'

'Where does your grandfather live?' asked William.

'On the other side of the border.'

'What ... you mean the Free State?'

James Pius nodded, but said no more. The less others knew these days he thought, the better. In any event there was no way William would want to hear about an old Republican.

Originally from Limerick, his grandfather was one of those who had refused to accept the division of Ireland. His Republicanism was rooted in the writings of Patrick Pearse. Partition, he regarded as a sell-out; those who accepted it as quislings. The job, he would say, had only been half done, and over the years he had seen to it that his son Ned, and in their turn Ned's sons, did their part to ensure that some day the job would be finished.

'Do you see that rainbow, James Pius?' he had said one day as they fished from the stone bridge not far from his home. 'Some day the British will be driven out of Ireland, and then unity will come. Just like that rainbow, it will touch both parts of the country and bring them together. Yes, that'll be the day. Ireland, united, Gaelic and free. I just hope I live to see it, that's all.'

But one of James Pius's brothers didn't live to see it.

While his grandfather's home was just south of the border, James Pius's family lived north of it. They were, therefore, a family geographically divided by the border, a family to whom that invisible line drawn by the British so long ago meant nothing and everything. But above all, they were a family to whom the presence of the British had become intolerable. To them, it seemed, nothing had changed; British soldiers, whose activities in the South in years gone by had been opposed by other generations, were still raiding the homes of Irish people in the North. They were still telling Irish people what they could and could not do in their own country, where they could and could not go, what flags they could or could not fly, even, on occasion, what songs they could or could not sing.

37

In such a situation, therefore, his grandfather's cottage just a few miles down the road was an island of freedom, a place where members of James Pius's family could meet friends, listen to the fiddle, sing ballads and rebel songs, but above all, meet friends ... friends in the movement. Once it had been a 'safe' house, a house where someone on the run could find refuge, but no more. His grandfather was too well known now for that. However, it was still a place where people could meet — and plan.

As the troubles dragged on, however, James Pius had seen his family north of the border disintegrate. Paddy, his eldest brother, had been forced to flee to America, although he was still raising money and wasn't entirely lost to the cause. His brothers Sean and Mick were doing life in the Maze Prison in County Antrim, while his big sister, Sis, was in the women's prison at Maghaberry not far from the Maze. And if all that wasn't enough, his brother Seamus had been shot dead ....

It was at that precise moment in James Pius's thoughts that the shot rang out and the bullet ricocheted off the boulders in front of the Hawk. He jumped, thinking for a moment that the shot was meant for him. Then, realising he was a sitting target, he scrambled to his feet, and with the boat tucked under his arm took to his heels. William immediately picked up the control box, and throwing a frightened look back at the hill where the shot had come from took off after him.

From behind the boulders, the Professor watched them go. He knew that once more the small plastic starfish inside the boat was flicking madly and that a sudden jolt could push it that hair's breadth further. If that happened, the bomb would go off and the boys would be dead. He took a deep breath, for he knew that valuable and all as he was to the organisation he would be lucky to survive the wrath of the Hawk.

Striker, meanwhile, had left his commando pack with his patrol, and like a panther stalking its prey set off through the woods on his own to reconnoitre the area.

When he returned a short time later, he reprimanded Brown and Mannering who were lying beneath their camouflage nets in the undergrowth some distance out from the remainder of the patrol. He had taken great care to position them in such a way that they could give advance warning of an attack; however, he had slipped past them, and wasn't amused.

'If I had been the bleeding Hawk, you'd be dead,' he told them. 'Now keep alert — and stay alive.'

He joined Smith and Peacock who were lying against an earthen embankment on the side of a low hill and they weren't surprised to find he had brought his own radio set with him. They knew that if he was operating out here on his own, he would have to have one stashed away somewhere.

Leaving his radio aside, Striker leaned against the embankment and trained his binoculars on the two boys. 'They're going to blow themselves to bits if they're not careful.'

'Why are you so sure there's a bomb in the boat?' asked Peacock.

Striker turned to face him, and Peacock felt the sergeant's eyes boring into him. He also noticed for the first time that the eyes between the dark green stripes of cam cream were brown, a very dark brown that seemed to act like an impenetrable wall behind which all feelings and emotions were carefully guarded.

'Use your head, Peacock,' he replied. 'You don't think the Hawk was sending it over for us to play with?'

'But how do you know it's not Semtex, Sarge?' asked Smith.

'Well, if it's new it's not Semtex, and if it's small enough to fit into a model boat it's certainly not Annie.'

39

Seeing the questioning look in their young faces, Striker said, 'How long have you two been in Northern Ireland?'

'Three weeks,' Peacock replied.

Striker turned his eyes up to heaven. Of all the soldiers available in the British Army, why did they have to saddle him with newcomers? Even a little bit of experience would have helped. But no, it had to be newcomers.

'Annie,' he told them, 'is a big fat lady who wears strong perfume and just be careful you don't step on her toes, because she's got one helluva punch.'

Realising that his sarcasm was wasted as they didn't know what he was talking about, he explained as patiently as he could. 'Annie is a home-made explosive which PIRA use. They make it by mixing a chemical called nitrobenzene with a fertiliser called ammonium nitrate. That's why we call it Annie — Ammonium Nitrate Northern Ireland Explosive.'

'Is it any good?' asked Smith.

'It's as powerful as Semtex, but not as handy.'

'Why's that, Sergeant?' asked Peacock.

'Because nitrobenzene is a liquid which they have to transport in bulk. It can be dangerous if you inhale it, and it stinks to high heaven, which is a dead giveaway.'

'So if it's not Semtex and it's not big Annie, it must be something special.' Peacock turned to peer through his rifle sight at the model boat. 'Why don't we just go down then and get it?'

'Because the Hawk is after it too, and if we play our cards right, we'll get him and the boat.' Striker took up his binoculars and trained them on a hill some distance away that was covered in grey-white rock and hazel bushes. 'Smith, you keep your eyes skinned and if you see any movement that might be the Hawk and his men, any movement at all, let me know.'

Striker crept back to where Willoughby was and asked him to make radio contact with two units which, they had been informed, had now been dropped into position several miles back in order to relay their messages to base, and provide reinforcements if necessary.

Peacock snuggled the side of his face into his Enfield rifle and tried to make himself comfortable with it. He found it difficult to get accustomed to this new short-barrelled weapon. The SA80 it was called, the SA being for small arms. A far cry, he thought, from the old wooden-stocked Lee Enfield, or the self-loading rifle that they had been using until now. At least, he thought, with the SLR there was plenty of barrel out in front, and somehow that was reassuring.

'What do you think?' he asked Smith.

'About what?'

'The new rifle.'

Smith peered through the sight of his own rifle, as if he was doing so for the first time. 'I think it's fine. Why, what's wrong with it?'

'I don't know. Somehow the barrel seems very short.'

'All they've done,' Smith explained,' is take the barrel and wrap the gun around it so as to give a lighter, more compact rifle.'

'Still, it's a smaller calibre weapon,' said Peacock.

'Smaller, but effective. All armies in the west are switching over to smaller calibre rifles now.'

'How do you think ours will match up to the guns the Hawk and his men have — if there's a fight to the finish?'

'No problem.' Smith adjusted the bipod on which his rifle rested. 'We've already hit one of them. And this little lady of mine will reach just that little bit farther than the rest.'

'What do you think they have?' asked Peacock.

Smith didn't look up. 'Armalites ... Kalashnikovs ... probably Kalashnikovs. They got a lot of them from Libya.'

Striker came over and knelt down beside them. He had heard what they had said, and knew Peacock was thinking of the formidable reputation the Kalashnikov had as a powerful, durable rifle, so he told them, 'A gun is only as good as the man who uses it. PIRA haven't a hope against trained soldiers, and the British soldier is the best trained soldier in the world. Don't forget that.' He looked at the hills beyond and continued, 'As for the Hawk, all he's got going for him is his reputation, and with a bit of luck we'll knock that into a cocked hat.'

'Look, Sarge,' whispered Smith urgently. 'There's something moving about, over there on that hill . . .'

Striker whipped his field-glasses up to his eyes. 'Where?'

'Behind the rocks, near the top of the hill.'

'It's the Hawk! Damn him, he's out of range.'

Smith shuffled to make himself more comfortable and pressed his eye closer to his times-four optical sight. 'I don't know, Sarge. I might just be able to hit him.'

'You'll never do it. He's out of range.'

'They're making a move, Sarge. What do you want me to do?'

Striker was still looking through the glasses. 'Fire one aimed shot. If you hit him so much the better. But at least it'll let him know he's not getting that boat back.'

Smith took careful aim and fired. As he did so, they could hear the bullet ricocheting off a rock on the opposite side of the hill and whining off into the distance.

Striker saw the Hawk and his men diving for cover and grunted with satisfaction. Then he switched his glasses to the two boys, and seeing them sprinting away with the boat, told his men, 'Come on, let's go.'

Chapter Five

'That flag's got to go!'

James Pius sat up. 'What flag?'

William pointed to the Tricolour on the stern of the model boat. 'That flag.'

Having run until they were once again exhausted, they had taken off their jackets and thrown themselves down on the bank of a river.

Now, as they recovered, William stared at the small Tricolour on the *Erin go Bragh*. He thought of what James Pius had called him — a black Prod. He thought of the IRA and he thought of his Uncle Robert. He had told James Pius he was hiking, but that wasn't strictly true. In a way he was, but it wasn't just a ramble through the hills. What he was doing was learning how to survive. Survive people like James Pius; people like those who had fired on them back at the lake, the IRA gunmen whom he and his family had come to fear on their isolated border farm.

Theirs was a fairly big place. It was a dairy farm and included some of the best land in the district. Two brothers, his father and his Uncle Robert, had inherited it from their parents. When his father had got married, they had both continued to live in the same big grey house, sharing the work of looking after their herd of Friesians.

It was hard work. The cows had to be milked morning and evening, every day without fail. As his father often said, there was no such thing as a five-day week for the cows or

43

the people who looked after them. As a result, they only went out one day of the week as a family, and that was to the local parish church on Sunday morning. On other occasions — even at holiday time — the two men had to take turns. It was the same when the marching season came around. Both were members of the Orange Order but only one paraded on the Twelfth of July, and that was his father. His Uncle Robert waited until the following day and walked with members of the Royal Black Preceptory.

William had, therefore, grown up into a family that was both Protestant and Unionist; a family that lived with its back to, and turned its back on, the Republic, a country that was foreign to them in all things religious and political. He had also found himself in a family that lived in fear.

It was a fear that arose not only from the remoteness of their situation, but from the fact that Uncle Robert was also a part-time member of the Ulster Defence Regiment. For as the troubles continued, a growing number of people were being killed by the IRA because of their support for the regiment. Many of them were part-time members, ambushed on lonely border roads and farms, people who, like Uncle Robert, considered it their duty to do occasional patrols with the regiment in spite of their commitments at home.

The conflict was claiming other lives too, Catholics as well as Protestants, but with each new attack on members of the security forces, particularly the UDR, William and his family felt more and more threatened. Who would be next? they wondered. Would it be them? And how would it happen? A bomb under the car? A fusilade of shots from the trees as they arrived home?

It was a fear that was with them all the time, and even though they lived in the wide open space of the farm, it was a fear that crept in around them so that sometimes they felt as if they were living in a prison.

Every time they took out the car, or even the tractor, they

had to go through the ritual of checking underneath in case the IRA had attached a bomb to it. Every time they heard the sound of a car coming up the laneway, they would look up and wonder if this was it.

Not surprisingly, however, the nights were the worst. The police didn't come around at night-time — it was too dangerous — and so their feeling of isolation was complete. When the dogs barked or grew restless, they would look at each other. No one would speak, but the same unspoken question was clearly etched on each and every face. Who was it? Friend or foe? Then Uncle Robert would take up the loaded revolver that he always kept near at hand and wait for the knock on the door. 'Who is it?' Spoken from the side in case shots might come splintering through the woodwork. Uncle Robert, revolver at the ready now, waiting. 'It's only a neighbour.' 'Thank God.' A sigh of relief. The gun back in its place, still loaded and within arm's reach. Safe for the moment.

On a dairy farm, however, they couldn't lock themselves in all night. There was the calving to attend to and somehow it always seemed to happen in the middle of the night. Then the darkness held more dangers than ever before, for the man working to bring new life to his herd was a perfect target in the light of the shed for those who sought to bring death and destruction.

Perhaps in the daytime they breathed a little easier. The daylight, the wide open spaces, always pushed back the barriers of fear just that little bit farther. Still, Uncle Robert never failed to take his revolver with him, even when he was driving the tractor out to one of the far fields. However, he didn't reckon on the fact that he might not come face to face with his attackers. It was a burst of rifle-fire that killed him. Nobody saw who fired it, probably not even Uncle Robert. He had no time to use his revolver. Not that it would have done him any good.

They didn't even hear the shots at home. It was only when the collie came home bloodied and whimpering that their worst fears were confirmed. They found the tractor in a ditch, Uncle Robert slumped over the wheel, his life-blood — not black but red and warm like everyone else's — draining away to mix with the tractor oil in the mud and slime at the bottom of the ditch.

The IRA issued a statement saying that they killed him because he was in the UDR. They needn't have bothered. Everyone knew who killed him and why. Their Catholic neighbours sympathised with them, and they were genuine. The priests condemned the killers, and they were genuine too. But then the priests also said Requiem Mass for the paramilitaries ... paramilitaries like the ones who killed Uncle Robert, and that was difficult to understand.

After that, an army man came and gave certain advice on safety measures they should take. William's father also decided that his son should learn the elementary skills of survival. The idea was that he should learn how to survive on his own, away from home, in case the situation arose where he had to take to the hills at short notice.

William, therefore, saw his present situation as a test, and in spite of the shooting was determined to stay where he was until the ownership of the *Erin go Bragh* was resolved.

He was still looking at the Tricolour on the stern of the boat. 'It's got to go,' he said.

'That flag,' James Pius told him firmly, 'happens to be my flag. It also happens to be on my half of the boat. So it's staying where it is!'

'What do you mean, your half of the boat?'

'I mean the half I got my hand to first.'

'Well, I got my hand to the other half first,' said William, 'so I've as much right to it as you!'

James Pius got up, saying, 'We'll soon see about that.'

William, however, was nearer the boat, and grabbed it.

'What do you think you're doing?' demanded James Pius.

'I'm going to mark out my half, that's what I'm doing.'

James Pius sat down. Since William had possession of the boat for the moment, there wasn't much he could do, and he was too warm and tired to start a wrestling match. So he just said, 'You can mark what you like. But it's my boat. I told you, I got my hand to it first.'

'You said half of it was yours,' said William. 'That means the other half of it is mine.' Placing the boat between his knees, he reached over and, unbuttoning the left breast pocket of his combat jacket, took out a tobacco tin with an olive-green lid.

James Pius watched with growing interest. The rectangular lid of the tobacco tin, he could see, was taped around with yellow tape. On the lid itself he could just make out the words "Golden Virginia", with the maker's name — W.D & H.O. Wills — underneath.

William peeled off the tape which he used to make sure the lid stayed on, opened the box and took out the stub of a yellow pencil.

A strange sweet smell came to James Pius's nostrils, not the smell of tobacco as he might have expected. Nevertheless, he sniggered and said, 'I thought for a minute there you were going to have a smoke to steady your nerves.'

Ignoring him, William lifted the boat and, gauging the half-way mark, drew a line right around it. Then he put the pencil back in the box, taped the lid on and returned it to his jacket pocket.

James Pius grunted as if to say he could draw all the lines he wanted, but the boat was still his. Privately, however, he was happy that the Tricolour was still there and that William had accepted its presence, albeit on the other side of the line.

Satisfied with his work, William put the boat back beside the control box. He didn't say so to James Pius, but he wasn't finished yet. Instead, he asked, 'Where do you think we are?'

James Pius shrugged. 'I'm not sure.'

'You mean you don't know?'

'I didn't say that.' James Pius ran his fingers through his wavy black hair, now tousled from all the running. 'When I have a look around I'll soon get my bearings.'

'Anyway,' said William, 'it doesn't matter if we are lost. I've a compass.' He looked at James Pius, now more distrustful of him than ever. Somehow he had the notion that it was easy for Catholics to tell lies, as all they had to do was confess to the priest and it was all right. Lying back, he rested his head in his cupped hands and said as casually as he could, 'I tell you what so. Why don't you go and see if you can get your bearings? I'll stay here and mind the boat.'

James Pius gave a loud guffaw, then pushing his foot over towards him said, 'Here, pull the other one.'

'Don't worry,' William assured him. 'I won't run off with it. I promise.' When James Pius laughed, he put his right hand up and told him, ' I swear. Anyway, where would I go? I don't know where we are.'

James Pius looked at him. He had always heard that Protestants didn't tell lies, and somehow he got the feeling that William wasn't telling him a lie now. 'All right,' he said finally. 'But I won't be far away. I'll just go back up through the woods and see if I can see anything from the top of the hill.'

'Don't worry. I'll still be here. And so will the boat.' William closed his eyes. He could sense James Pius watching him for a few seconds; then he heard him making his way somewhat reluctantly up through the trees. Even then he didn't move, for he felt James Pius would stop and watch him for a while, just in case he made a run for it with the boat. It was only when he was fairly sure he was no longer being watched that he sat up, took out his tobacco box again and opened it.

This time William took a Wilkinson Sword razor-blade from the box and, lifting his combat jacket, proceeded to slit the stitches on the label which bore a Union Jack. Placing the blade and the label in the upturned lid, he rooted in the box once more until he found three needles wrapped in brown thread. Unwinding the thread, he extracted one of the needles, threaded it and sewed the label on to the top of the aerial that protruded from the front right corner of the cabin of the *Erin go Bragh*. Then he took out the stub of the pencil and etched the words 'Ulster Says No' on each side of the bow.

Having admired his handiwork, William turned his attention to the control box. The boat, he reckoned, was no good without it. Therefore, if he had the box he would be holding a trump card when it came to deciding who owned the boat. He could hear James Pius coming back now, so he quickly put the control box into one of the larger inside pockets of his jacket and lay back again.

'Well?' he asked, when James Pius returned.

'Well what?'

'Did you find out where we are?'

'Not exactly.' James Pius eyed him suspiciously. 'I thought you'd have been well on your way by now.'

William sat up. 'I gave you my word, didn't I?'

Still suspicious, James Pius glanced at the boat. He immediately spotted the Union Jack and the slogan of loyalist opposition to the Anglo-Irish Agreement. 'You sneak,' he spat out. 'And I thought you lot never told lies.'

'I didn't tell a lie. I said I wouldn't run off with it, and neither I did.'

'No, but look what else you did when my back was turned.' James Pius stepped forward. 'Well, I'm telling you no word of a lie. All that rubbish is coming off it.'

William jumped to his feet to restrain him, and next moment they were wrestling furiously in the long grass.

'There'll be no Union Jack on my boat!' panted James Pius. 'And no unionist slogans either.'

William threw him over and, as he looked down at him, gritted his teeth and told him, 'That's on my half of the boat, remember? I can put whatever I like on it.'

Throwing him off, James Pius reached for the boat, only to be bowled off his feet as William rushed at him head on.

On a hillside overlooking the river, the members of the IRA active service unit watched and held their breath.

'Well, Professor,' said Sean the Hawk, 'what do you think?'

'It's touch and go. A good kick could set it off. It all depends.'

'Depends on what.'

'On what way they have the switches and controls ... how hard they kick it.'

Sean the Hawk turned and pushing the muzzle of his Kalashnikov up under the Professor's chin told him, 'Well, then, you just better pray that they don't kick it.'

From another vantage point, Striker was also watching the tussle down at the river. He too was praying that the boys wouldn't accidentally detonate the bomb. If they did, he would never find out what was in it. They would also shatter whatever hope he had of catching the Hawk.

Fortunately, neither Striker nor the Hawk need have worried. James Pius and William were still too weary to put up more than a token struggle, and after rolling about for a minute or two, both fell back exhausted. Each had accepted, for the moment at any rate, the presence of a foreign flag — and an equally foreign slogan — on the other side of that thin grey line.

Chapter Six

The sun was now low in the sky. William got up, walked back to the trees and began to examine them.

Wondering what he was up to, James Pius followed him. 'What are you doing?'

'I'm going to build a shelter.'

'What for?'

William turned and looked at James Pius. 'Look, there's no way we're going to find out where we are before dark. That means we'll have to spend the night here.'

James Pius wasn't sure if William was serious or if this was another ploy. 'What do you need a shelter for? Sure it's a lovely summer's evening.'

William took the tobacco tin out of his jacket pocket. 'It is now. But it can get cold at night, and if it gets windy or wet it's better to have a shelter.'

It was a British army expert who had shown William some of the basic means of survival.

'To survive,' the officer had told him, 'you must set yourself a list of priorities — safety of location, shelter, water, food. Once you've established these, you can decide what course of action to take.'

So far as the location was concerned, William reckoned it couldn't be better. The trees would provide protection, the river water and food.

James Pius came over as he was hanging his jacket on the branch of a tree. 'What's in that box anyway?'

'It's a survival kit. It contains everything I need to survive out in the open.'

James Pius gave him a scornful look. 'That's impossible. You couldn't have everything you need in that small box.'

'It would surprise you what I have in there.' William untaped the lid and stuck the end of the tape to the bark of the tree. James Pius could see the box was packed full of odds and ends. 'That's my compass,' William told him, taking out a black object no bigger than the large button of an overcoat.

James Pius watched the points of the compass, which were marked in silver, moving around gently until they settled. 'What's that funny sweet smell?'

'That's an insect repellant. It's handy if flies are annoying you, especially clegs.'

'And what's that there?' asked James Pius, pointing to a coil of silvery wire with two silvery rings on each end.

'A wire saw.' William demonstrated by taking hold of the rings and pulling it back and forth across a piece of dead wood. 'Now I'm going to build a shelter. Are you going to give me a hand?'

James Pius snorted. 'You must be out of your mind.' However, he could see now that William was serious about spending the night there. Not to worry, he thought. His grandfather wasn't expecting him, so if he had to stay out overnight it wouldn't cause any problem. His family wouldn't know he hadn't arrived, and his grandfather wouldn't know he was coming.

Having selected two trees which were growing close together at the edge of the wood, William used the small wire saw to cut down a long ash pole. This he pushed down into the Y-shaped forks formed by the lowest branches of the two trees so that it was suspended between them like the crossbar of a goalpost, only much lower. Satisfied that the pole was firmly in position, he then cut a number of other branches

52

and leaned them against the first one.

James Pius watched with a mixture of amusement and curiosity but said nothing. He was also biding his time, as he had noticed that the control box was missing, and knew there was only one place it could be.

Using the sleeves of his jacket to protect his hands, William now pulled a bundle of nettles, laid them across a stone, and proceeded to pulverise them with another stone. Then he took the stringy bits and used them to bind the frame of the shelter together. At this stage, James Pius concluded that his black Protestant friend was definitely mad. However, he said nothing.

'I'm going to light a fire now,' said William when he had finished. 'The least you could do is collect some wood.'

Whatever about anything else, James Pius thought they might need a fire, so he went off and gathered any dry twigs and rotten branches he could find.

When he returned, he found that William had collected enough stones to make a circle for the fire just outside the shelter. They were wet, and realising they had come from the river, he asked, 'What do you think you're doing with them?'

'I'm using them to build a fire,' William replied.

'You can't use stones from the river to build a fire.'

'Why not?'

James Pius glared at him. 'Because they're full of water. They'll explode with the heat!'

William was taken aback. That was something the officer hadn't mentioned. 'Who told you that?' he asked.

'My grandfather. We sometimes light a fire when we go fishing.' However, James Pius didn't say where his grandfather had learned his survival techniques. He hadn't said so in so many words, but James Pius gathered he had learned his fieldcraft when he was on the run.

Having helped William to throw the stones back into the

river and collect new ones, he said, 'I suppose you have a match in your magic box?'

William nodded.

'And what happens if your matches get wet?'

'Then I use my flint and steel.' William showed him a small bit of wood with a short piece of hacksaw blade embedded in one edge and a bar of flint in the other. Removing the blade, he struck the saw edge down along the flint, producing a spectacular shower of sparks. 'Anyway, I don't need it now. The matches are dry.'

Returning the flint and steel to the box, William took out a match and a piece of cottonwool. He tucked the cottonwool under a small pile of dry twigs, put the match to it and in next to no time had a fire going. 'Now,' he said, 'see if you can keep it going. I have to finish the shelter.'

James Pius watched William cover the branches of the shelter with clusters of large lime and sycamore leaves. He didn't like the way he had taken the control box, probably thinking he wouldn't notice. Now he watched him lift the *Erin go Bragh* and place it carefully inside the shelter, and he didn't like the way he did that either. It was almost as if he thought he owned that too. The control box, he reckoned, was in the jacket, which was still hanging up on a nearby tree. There was no hope of getting that, at least not for the moment. At any rate, it was no good without the boat. On the other hand, the boat was still a boat, even without the control box. What he needed was time to figure out a way to get it for himself.

As James Pius thought about these things, his eyes focussed on the Union Jack that hung from the aerial of the *Erin go Bragh*. How he hated that flag and everything it stood for. He thought of his family and everything they had gone through to try and get rid of it ... and he thought of his brother Seamus who had been killed by the forces who served under it.

54

'And here am I,' he said to himself, 'sharing a fire with a Protestant who has the affrontery to put a Union Jack on my boat and say that half of it belongs to him.'

Suddenly, for no reason that he knew, he started to sing:

> *Sinne Fianna Fáil,*
> *Atá faoi gheall ag Éirinn,*
> *Buíon dár slua*
> *Thar toinn do ráinig chughainn*
> *Faoi mhóid bheith saor.*
> *Seantír ár sinsear feasta*
> *Ní fhágfar faoin tíorán ná faoin tráill;*
> *Anocht a théam sa bhearna bhaoil . . .*

William came over and sat down beside him. 'What are you blethering about?'

'That, in case you don't know it, is *The Soldier's Song.*'

'How would I know what it is? It's in a foreign language.'

Amazed that William didn't know it, James Pius launched into a few lines in English by way of translation :

> *In Erin's cause come woe or weal*
> *'Mid canon's roar or rifles peal*
> *We'll chant the soldiers song. . .*

Seeing he was wasting his time, James Pius stopped singing and looked at William. 'It's the National Anthem.'

'All I know is, *The Soldier's Song* is the national anthem of the Free State, and it sounds like a war song to me.' William shook his head. 'But you know, you lot will never learn. You think because there's a wee bit of orange in your flag you can force a million Protestants to accept it. Then you stand in front of it and sing an anthem in a language we can't understand. And you talk about a United Ireland! Anyway, there's only one anthem we recognise and that's *God Save the Queen.*'

With that, William launched into a rendering of the British

national anthem, whereupon James Pius, not to be out-done, resumed his rendering of *The Soldier's Song*.

Up in the hills, Sean the Hawk and his men, and Striker and his men, listened to the singing and wondered what was going on.

Chapter Seven

Of all Striker's men, Mannering was probably the most thoughtful. Mild Mannering he was called by his mates in the car plant back in England where he worked before joining the army. However, behind that studious look and quiet manner, was a heart that yearned for adventure. He was well read on matters military, took an intelligent interest in all the briefings he got and enjoyed soldiering to the full. It wasn't surprising, therefore, when Striker asked for a volunteer that he stepped forward.

It had become increasingly obvious to Mannering and his friends that Striker was no ordinary soldier. He was superbly fit, never seemed to tire under a very full pack, carried night vision and other specialised equipment, and seemed to be a law unto himself. While he wore the same cap badge as they did, they had also concluded that he was not a member of their regiment.

Most likely, they thought, Striker was an SAS man, a member of the 22 Special Air Service Regiment, the most elite unit in the British Army. Neither of his forearms bore the famous winged dagger of the SAS with its equally famous motto, *Who Dares Wins*. In fact, his arms bore no tattoos at all. That was something they found most unusual for a soldier, but then, as they thought about it, they reckoned it was just one more indication that he belonged to a regiment that was also the most secretive.

Having reconnoitred the woods overlooking the river

where the boys had come to a stop, Striker had established two observation posts, or OP's as they were known, so that they wouldn't be taken unawares by the Hawk.

'Where do you think he is?' asked Peacock.

Striker produced a detailed map of the area and, spreading it on the ground, told them, 'We're here. The boys are there. Now while we're looking across the river at them, because of the way it twists and turns between the hills, we're actually on the same side of it as they are.'

'And the Hawk?' asked Willoughby.

'Well, if he's as anxious to get his bomb back as I think he is, he's still watching the boys, which means he isn't very far away. And if I know him, he'll be doing that from the other side of the river.'

'How come?' asked Mannering.

'Because the river forms the border, and he takes good care to stay on the other side of it — when it suits him.'

'Which means we can't touch him,' said Peacock.

Striker looked at him and for a moment his dark brown eyes flickered with the slightest hint of a smile, as if to say, Don't be so naïve. 'What it means is we have to make bloody sure we don't get caught on the wrong side of the river, or Dublin would raise hell at the Anglo-Irish Conference.' He paused. 'But that's not to say we can't go over and ruffle his feathers a little!'

When Mannering offered to go, Striker told him to leave his back-pack, his pouches of food and his water bottle with Willoughby and Peacock. All he needed was his rifle and ammunition.

Willoughby would keep an ear to the radio and an eye on the river, Peacock would watch the boys, while Smith and Brown, who were manning the OP's, would maintain a high state of alert to make sure they weren't caught off guard. If they heard firing, on no account were they to respond, unless, of course, Mannering and he required covering fire as they returned across the river.

'Would you not take your own radio, Sarge?' asked Willoughby. 'At least we'd know what was going on.'

Striker shook his head, and picking up his rifle said, 'No, we'll travel light. That way we'll have a better chance of getting back out.'

Mannering glanced at the others, but if he was having second thoughts he said nothing.

When they had gone, Peacock peered at the two boys through the optic sight of his rifle. 'Never volunteer,' he said.

It was an old army maxim, and Willoughby agreed that it was sound advice. He watched Striker and Mannering give each other cover as they ran crouching across the shallows below. 'If they're caught they're in for it.'

'Mannering says a group of our SAS chaps were caught in the South once, and claimed they had made a map-reading error. Had to go to court in Dublin, but they got away with it.'

'No use saying it's a map-reading error this time,' said Willoughby.

Peacock nodded. 'Not with the river marking the border. And if they're caught, we're all in for it. They'll say you should have been on the blower to the OC.'

'Follow orders and ask no questions. That's what I've always been told,' Willoughby replied. 'And that's what I'm going to do.'

'Striker must be SAS,' said Peacock. 'What do you reckon?'

Willoughby watched as Striker and Mannering picked their way through the scrub and disappeared up into the woods on the far side of the river. 'Must be.'

'One of the boys is building a shelter,' Peacock observed. 'I'll tell you something ... I thought I was fit until I saw Striker take off after those two.'

'Mannering says the SAS selection course includes a forty

mile endurance march through the Brecon Beacons in Wales.'
Pausing to emphasise what he was going to say, Willoughby
added, 'With a 55-pound rucksack and a ten-pound rifle.'

'Rather them than me.'

'And it must be done in at least twenty hours,' continued
Willoughby. 'He says they're trained in the use of explosives,
jungle warfare and all sorts of things. That they eat worms
when they're short of food, and rats for their Christmas
dinner. Yuk! Can you imagine?'

In fact, once they had come to suspect Striker was an SAS
man, Mannering had related a lot of the things he had read
about the 22 Special Air Service Regiment ... how over a
period of two years candidates underwent sickening ordeals
which built up their physical and mental strength, and tested
them to the point of exhaustion. During combat survival
training, he said, they were sometimes left lying naked in the
snow for hours before being questioned, to test their
resistance to interrogation. And as for weapons training,
Mannering told them, there was nothing to equal 'the killing
house' at SAS Headquarters in Hereford. Formally known
as the Close Quarter Battle (CQB) House, it was there they
learned how to deal with hostage situations. Operating in
pairs, he said, they would burst into the rooms which
contained dummies representing terrorists and hostages, and
rolling across the floor, hit each terrorist with two shots
known as a 'double tap' from a 13-round 9mm Browning
pistol ...

What Mannering didn't tell them was that secretly he
nursed the ambition to become an SAS man himself one day.
Every time he thought of the SAS, he recalled the television
pictures of the deadly efficient way in which the shadowy
figures of the regiment had brought an end to the siege at
the Iranian Embassy in London in 1980. He had read of their
daring exploits in the jungles of Malaya and Borneo, in the
burning sands of Aden and Oman, and on the misty crags

60

of the Falklands. More recently, he had heard of their activities in Northern Ireland, where they were sometimes brought in to ambush terrorists, then whisked away by helicopter before anyone could ask any questions. The dogs of war, their critics called them, but how he wished he could join them.

Volunteering to go with Striker was, therefore, no act of heroism on his part, but a welcome opportunity to see how the SAS Regiment worked and even to be part of it.

Shortly after crossing the river, Striker and Mannering moved from tree to tree to check out the immediate area. It was clear. Continuing to use trees as cover, they then edged their way up to the brow of the hill and into the woods beyond. There Striker instructed Mannering to conceal himself at a point where he could see between the trees for some distance, and set off in a wide circle to reconnoitre the area on his own.

As he lay in the undergrowth, Mannering now became aware of that lonely, almost timeless feeling one gets beneath tall trees as they nod and sway in the wind. Somehow it made him feel more alone than he had ever felt in his life before, and he wondered how he found himself in such a situation. Here he was in enemy territory, and the Hawk for whose blood the whole of Britain was screaming was probably somewhere nearby. A wrong move, and either the Hawk would kill him or he would be arrested. In either event, the Army would disown him. Perhaps those who said 'Never volunteer' were right. Then he thought of the SAS motto, *Who Dares Wins*, and told himself he must put such thoughts aside.

Changing the lever on the left side of his rifle butt from single shot to automatic, he pulled back the cocking handle and scanned the woods ahead of him. Whatever the rights or wrongs of the situation, he wasn't going to be found wanting. 'Shoot first, ask questions later,' he said to himself.

'Whoever's going to be killed, it's not going to be me.'

As the minutes ticked by, Mannering waited patiently for Striker's return. Suddenly, to his surprise, he noticed a flurry of furry bodies rolling about on the ground about a hundred metres ahead. Squinting through his optic sight, he could see that they were animals of some sort. Probably foxes, he thought. Being a city boy, born and bred, he didn't know much about animals and wasn't sure, and in the way that city people can feel frightened in the wide open spaces of the country, he felt scared. Perhaps it was because he had never seen wild animals at such close quarters before. He had a strong urge to get up and go back to the river. However, the thought of Striker's wrath scared him even more, so he lay still and held his breath. After a while, the foxes, or whatever they were, stopped rolling around; one of them ran off and the others dashed after it.

After what seemed an eternity, Striker slipped in beside him. 'Well,' he whispered. 'Any move?'

Mannering shook his head. 'Not a thing, except for foxes, and they'd hardly be there if there was anyone else around.'

Striker nodded. 'What were they doing?'

'Rolling around ... probably fighting over food.'

'Show me.'

Mannering was surprised that Striker should be so interested in wildlife, especially at a time like this, but he did as he was told.

Kneeling at the spot where the foxes had been, Striker examined the ground. 'You're right. They were fighting over food. Bread!' Carefully he pushed aside the undergrowth. 'It must have been buried in here.'

'The Hawk?'

Striker nodded. 'Probably buried their scraps. Good thinking, but not good enough. Didn't bury them deep enough.' He ran his fingers over the ground in an ever widening circle. 'And I wonder what else they've buried?'

62

Taking out his commando knife, he gently probed the soil with it. 'Ah, something soft. A rucksack maybe.' Carefully he pulled the soft soil away with his fingers. 'Just as I thought!'

'What is it?' asked Mannering, who was trying to see what Striker was doing, while keeping an eye on the surrounding woods.

Still exercising the greatest care, Striker lifted out the rucksack and opened it. 'I'd say it's the Hawk's store of bomb-making materials. Now wasn't that worth coming over for?'

Mannering watched as Striker removed the contents of the rucksack — three packets on which the words EXPLOSIVE PLASTIC SEMTEX-H were clearly printed, an entanglement of wires, nylon fishing-line, batteries, and a piece of plywood about six inches square, to which someone had taped a clothes-peg. 'What's that for?' he asked.

As Striker held up the piece of plywood, Mannering could see that two thumb tacks had been pressed into each lip of the peg, and a wire lead soldered to each of them. Striker located a small piece of plastic, the size of a stamp, to which someone had tied a piece of fishing-line, opened the peg, and inserted it between the thumb tacks. 'That,' he said, 'is one of the Hawk's nasty little booby-traps. He strings the nylon line across a path, or among the bushes, and hopes that you'll walk into it. If you do, you pull out the piece of plastic, the metal tacks make contact, and BOOM! You're back in civvy street. That is, if you're still alive.'

'What are you going to do with it?'

Striker set the piece of plywood with its deadly clothes-peg on the ground, saying, 'You take cover ... same place as before, and keep a sharp look out for the Hawk. I'll rig this up and see if we can't give him a dose of his own medicine.'

Returning to his original position beneath the undergrowth, Mannering watched as Striker connected up the wires and batteries, strung the nylon trip-wire around the trees, and carefully inserted the small piece of plastic into the clothes-peg.

A few moments later, Striker ran, crouching, back to join him. 'Now,' he said, 'you stay here. I'll take up position just over there, and let's hope the bomb does its work. If it doesn't, you know what to do.'

Time passed, and still there was no sign of the Hawk. Mannering grew restless. More than once he looked over towards Striker, but couldn't see him. The only thing he saw was a young fox. Thinking they were gone, it had ventured back. He looked at it through his rifle sight. At the same time he heard the distant sound of singing. Must be the boys down at the river, he thought, and he wondered, almost absent-mindedly, what they had to sing about. The fox, he could see, had heard them too. It seemed wary, uncertain, and he wondered if it had a den nearby. But no, it was returning to see if it could dig up any more food!

Hardly had Mannering realised what the fox was up to than it touched Striker's trip-wire, triggering the booby-trap bomb. In the same instant, an ear-splitting explosion reverberated through the woods, showering him with stones and soil.

Striker was by his side almost before the last stones had fallen.

'If that doesn't bring the Hawk,' panted Mannering, 'nothing will.'

'Maybe, maybe not. He doesn't know who else it's going to bring, and neither do we.' Striker was kneeling on one knee, analysing the possibilities, and Mannering detected a glint in his dark brown eyes as he added, 'But one way or the other, he'll know we've been here. Now, let's go!'

Taking off through the woods as fast as they could, the two of them arrived back down at the river bank a few moments later.

'Keep going!' shouted Striker. 'I'll cover you until you get across.'

Hearing the explosion, Willoughby and Peacock both trained their rifles on the woods beyond the river.

'They're coming back,' said Peacock. 'Mannering's over.'

'And there's Striker,' said Willoughby. 'I wonder what they've been doing?'

'Beats me, but I don't see anyone coming after them.'

'Well, keep your eyes peeled,' warned Willoughby. 'And remember what Striker said. Don't fire unless they need cover.'

As it so happened, Sean the Hawk and his men weren't far away when the explosion occurred, and they realised immediately that some of their stores had gone up.

The Hawk also realised that only one person could have been responsible, and as he watched the smoke rising above the trees, he exclaimed, 'It's Striker!'

'Why don't we go after him?' suggested Cathal Óg.

'He'll be back across the river by now. Anyway, he could be trying to lead us into a trap.'

'The nerve of him,' gasped Seamus. 'Coming over here and blowing up our supplies. He must think he's in the bloody jungle!'

'Well, he'll soon learn he *is* in the jungle,' declared the Hawk. 'The Irish jungle. Come on. He may have got some of our Semtex, but he's not getting the stuff on the *Erin go Bragh*.'

Chapter Eight

James Pius and William were still singing at the top of their voices when the explosion occurred, and so loudly were they singing that they weren't quite sure for a moment what they had heard.

'What was that?' asked James Pius.

'Sounded like a bomb!' William pointed to a plume of grey-black smoke that was now rising from the far side of one of the surrounding hills. 'Look, over there.'

'Who'd be bombing down here?'

'The IRA,' said William. 'Who'd you think?'

James Pius gave him a scornful look. 'More likely the Brits blowing up another bridge.'

'Sure there are no roads over there. That's where we've just come from.'

'Doesn't have to be on a road. Could be a footbridge, or one a farmer uses. It doesn't matter to them whether people have to walk for miles to get around it.'

'Well, if it makes the terrorists walk for miles too, then it's a good thing that they are blown up,' said William.

'It's all right as long as it's not your footbridge and you don't have to do the walking,' declared James Pius. 'But what if you do your shopping on the other side of it.'

'If it was blown up,' said William, 'it was on the border, so people had no business coming over here to do their shopping. They should stay on their own side. But then, of course, they'd be getting things cheaper up here, wouldn't they? And maybe even doing a bit of smuggling.'

'What about it if they are?' asked James Pius.

'It's dishonest, that's what. And anyway, it's their own fault that things are so dear down there. If they'd stayed in the United Kingdom they'd just be as well off as we are.'

'Well, for your information, Smarty, there are people who live on this island who are not interested in taking the Queen's shilling.'

'No, but they don't mind taking a life, even if it's an Irish life.'

'Collaborators and informers,' declared James Pius. 'I wouldn't call them Irish. They're traitors.'

William stood up as he felt he might have to defend himself physically now. 'Is that so? Well it might interest you to know that the members of the RUC and UDR that the IRA kill are just as Irish as you are. The only difference is they don't want anything to do with the type of Ireland the IRA are trying to force them into.'

James Pius stood up too. 'If you Protestants are so Irish, why are you always bowing and scraping to the British?'

'We don't bow and scrape. We don't have to. We are British.'

'A minute ago you said you were Irish. You can't be both.'

'Why can't we?'

James Pius sat down again. 'If you're so loyal, how come you won't do what the British Government tells you to do? You wouldn't accept power-sharing with us, would you? Just because we're Catholics. And now you won't accept the Anglo-Irish Agreement.'

'We don't accept that a foreign government should have any say in the running of our country,' said William, 'and that's what the Free State is to us — a foreign country. Anyway, our loyalty is to the Queen, not to the British Government.'

'Aye,' sneered James Pius, 'a foreign queen.'

67

'She's not a foreign queen,' William declared. 'She's our Queen, and why shouldn't she be, just because she's English? Your loyalty is to the Pope, and he's Italian.'

'He's not Italian, he's Polish. Anyway, that's different.'

'Is it now? Well, I bet you didn't know the Pope said prayers for the success of King William at the Battle of the Boyne. I bet you didn't know that, did you?'

James Pius didn't know that, nor could he imagine it being true, so he just gave a disbelieving grunt and ignored it.

Seeing that he wasn't going to get a response, William looked in the direction where the explosion had occurred. Beyond it the sun was edging its way down towards the horizon. However, he didn't need that to tell him he was getting hungry. He walked over to the tree where his jacket was hanging and took out his "Golden Virginia" tobacco box.

'What are you going to do with your magic box now?' asked James Pius sarcastically. 'Send out an SOS for your Brit friends to come and get you?'

William came over, and sitting down beside him, said 'For your information, I'm going to try and get something we can eat. That is, if you don't mind taking something to eat from a black Protestant.'

James Pius watched as William opened the box. Once more he got that distinct sweet smell from its contents, and he could see the inside of the black button compass swivelling around.

From beneath cottonwool and various other objects, William took a policeman's whistle, around which was wrapped nylon fishing-line. He tied the end of the line to a stone, and and set about attaching fish-hooks to it at intervals. James Pius, he could see, was watching him with some amusement. 'The least you could do is dig up some worms as bait.'

'I've nothing to dig with.'

'Here.' William tossed his sheath knife over to him. 'And

68

be careful you don't break the blade.'

By the time William had finished tying on the hooks, his reluctant companion had unearthed enough worms for him. Carefully he attached these to the hooks, then gently tossed the stone into the river and tied the other end of the line to a small sally that grew precariously on the bank.

James Pius gave his hands a good wash, wiped them on his trousers, and lying down on one elbow watched William search around until he found a large plastic bottle which had drifted down the river. 'What are you going to do now?' he asked sarcastically. 'Give the fish a drink?'

Ignoring the sarcasm, William cut the top off the bottle from about three inches under the shoulder, inserted a stone into the bottom, and dropped in a handful of daisy petals. He then put the top part back so that the neck was facing inwards. 'That's to catch minnow for bait,' he explained. He pierced the main part of the bottle with the point of his knife. 'It acts like a lobster pot. The fish can get in, but they can't get out.'

'What's the idea of the daisy petals?'

'Bait. Anything white attracts them.'

'And what are the holes for?'

'To let the water through. The stone anchors it to the bottom.'

As William placed the bottle in shallow water not far from the bank, with the open end facing the current, James Pius extracted a small parcel from his jacket pocket, opened it and took out a sandwich. Taking a bite, he said, 'And when are we going to be eating all these fish?'

'Whenever we catch them.' William looked up. He was surprised, almost startled, to see James Pius eating a sandwich, but he tried not to show it. It had never occurred to him that James Pius might have brought food, and he could see he was not only enjoying it, but also relishing the look on his face.

'Here, have a sandwich — if you don't mind taking food from a teague.'

If James Pius's intention was to tease, it didn't work. William could see that he was playing games, but his was a much bigger game — the game of survival. He had been told that when it came to getting food, he should take it from whatever source it was available. So he just said 'Thanks,' and accepted the offer.

It was a ham sandwich, and he ate it hungrily. 'How many have you left?'

James Pius rolled up the paper and threw it away. 'None. That's the lot.'

William retrieved the paper. 'It's greasy. Ideal for lighting a fire.'

'How are you going to cook all these fish you're going to catch?'

'Probably on a spit. Why?'

James Pius gave a derisive laugh. 'That's not the way to cook a fish.'

'And how would you do it?'

James Pius shrugged. 'You just put a flat stone in the middle of the fire and cook it on that.'

'I suppose your grandfather told you that too?'

'As a matter of fact he did.'

William opened his box again, and taking out a copper wire snare said, 'All right. You see if you can find a flat stone. It might do for a fish. I'll set this and see if I can get a rabbit. We'll need a spit for that.'

James Pius brushed off the crumbs that had fallen on his clothes. 'Snares are illegal, you know.'

'Huh! That's a good one, coming from you.'

'Where did you get it?'

'I got it from a man in a shop near Enniskillen. When I told him what I wanted it for he went into the back and got it. Anyway, it's not illegal, not if it's a matter of survival.

70

Now, are you going to do what I ask or not?'

James Pius looked at him and then at the box which was lying open on the grass. 'Fair enough.'

William paused, wondering if he was thinking of getting his own back on him for putting the Union Jack on the *Erin go Bragh*. 'But promise you won't touch the boat.'

'I promise.'

'Or the flag.'

'I told you. I won't touch it.'

William looked at him, not at all sure he could trust him. Then he put on his jacket, saying, 'All right. I'll be back in a minute.'

In a nearby field, William walked parallel to a low embankment on which grew a hawthorn hedge. By looking directly into the embankment he could see a number of rabbit paths among the thistles, dock leaves and nettles.

Originally he had imagined that snares would be set at the entrance to rabbit burrows, but the officer who had taught him survival techniques had told him otherwise. The best place to put them, he had explained, was on the paths travelled by the rabbits to and from their burrows. But, there was more to it than that. Rabbits hopped when leaving their burrows, so the snare should be placed above ground.

James Pius, he could see, was still sitting on the river bank, so he searched around for a piece of stick to use as a peg. He knew the peg shouldn't be freshly broken or the rabbits would smell it, and not brittle or they would break it. What he needed was a short weathered stick that still had some strength in it. Having found a piece of hawthorn which he considered suitable, he attached the snare to it and pushed it into the ground behind a thistle. Growing as it was at the edge of a rabbit path, the thistle would hide the peg. He then opened the neck of the snare so that it was the width of four fingers, and twisted it up and around so that it stayed in position four fingers' width above the path. It might be next day before his scent had gone, but if the officer was right, he stood a good chance of snaring a rabbit.

James Pius sat on the river bank for several minutes after William had left. The *Erin go Bragh* was still under the shelter where they had left it, and as he eyed it he thought how that red, white and blue flag annoyed him. However, the green, white and orange was on it too. What was more, it flew from the stern where all ships' flags should fly; as far as he was concerned it was the real flag, the one that proclaimed the true nationality of the vessel.

He had noticed that William had taken care to take the jacket with him, confirming his suspicion that the control box was in one of the pockets, and once again he thought that the way William had quietly taken the box was even sneakier than what he had done to the boat.

The evening breeze brought the sweet smell of the tobacco box to his nostrils, and looking down he saw that it was lying open on the ground beside him. Having made sure William wasn't watching, he reached in among the various bits and pieces, took out the black button compass and put it in his pocket.

Without a compass William would remain lost for longer, and that, he reckoned, would give him the time he needed to figure out a way of getting the boat for himself.

'Now,' he said, 'we'll see just how smart he is.'

From a meadow on the opposite side of the river, Sean the Hawk watched as William rejoined James Pius. Through the tall swaying reeds that grew right up to the river's edge, he could see William lifting the *Erin go Bragh* and examining it before returning it to the shelter. Knowing that with Striker also watching the boat from the hills, it was going to be very difficult to retrieve it, he leaned back against the trunk of a sally bush and fingered his Kalashnikov rifle thoughtfully. Only now did he become aware of the silence of the meadow, a silence broken only by the rustle of the reeds, or *giolcacha* as they were known in Irish.

As he watched the purple seed heads rise and fall, he reflected for a moment on the campaign he had waged against what he bitterly considered to be the forces of British imperialism. Unlike the Professor, he was from the North, or the occupied Six Counties as he himself called them. He had grown up in the troubles, and saw himself as a member of a nationalist minority which, by the stroke of a British pen, had been corralled against their will into a small corner of Ireland with a loyalist majority.

While others considered it to be a political problem to be resolved within the confines of the border, to him the problem was the border. It was a border imposed by Britain and maintained by British troops. As far as he was concerned, the problem would never be solved until both were gone and Ireland was united. Talk, he believed, would never bring that about; the only thing Britain understood was what came from the barrel of a gun. Some day, he believed, the British connection would be broken, and then the IRA's ultimate goal, the establishment of an all-Ireland socialist republic, would be in sight.

The shipments of arms and explosives which Gadafy had sent from Libya had been the biggest boost to their campaign so far. But the Semtex wouldn't last forever, and Maggie Thatcher had raised such a clamour that the Czechs, who manufactured it, were under pressure to impose stricter controls on their exports. It was imperative, therefore, that they should come up with an alternative — and so they had.

However, things had gone wrong. There, across the river, was their alternative in the *Erin go Bragh*, with the Brits now watching it, determined to find out what they were up to. If the Brits succeeded, they would realise just what they had come up with, Maggie Thatcher would raise hell again, and the supply of chemicals would dry up before they even got started on production.

Now as the Hawk wondered how he was going to regain possession of the boat, he thought of the trouble they had taken to prepare it for its short voyage. Television pictures of the wreckage collected from the sea after the IRA had murdered Lord Mountbatten had been etched in his memory, especially shots of the piece bearing the name of Mountbatten's boat, *Shadow V*.

It was for that reason he had taken particular trouble to choose a name for his model boat. As well as carrying a bomb, he wanted it to carry a message. He had thought at first he might call it *The Hawk*, but decided that wasn't subtle enough. He then considered calling it *The Fenian Ram*. That was the name of the first real submarine ever built, and it was developed by a Clareman, John P. Holland, in the U.S., with financial support from the Fenian movement which was hoping to use submarines against England. However, he came to the conclusion that the significance of that would be wasted on the Brits. They were inclined to think that anything worthwhile was invented by them, and in spite of their long involvement in Ireland were, in his opinion, woefully ignorant of Irish history.

It was then he thought of calling it the *Erin go Bragh*. A keen student of the 1798 Rebellion, he had read that some of the leaders of that ill-fated attempt to establish the first Irish republic had displayed the motto *Erin go Bragh* in gold letters on their hats. Even the Brits, he reckoned, couldn't fail to know what that meant, and so he had painstakingly painted it in gold on the stern of the boat.

Striker wouldn't know what had hit him, but those who picked up the pieces would. *Erin go Bragh* — Ireland for Ever. They'd get the message all right, and they'd know who sent it.

However, the plan had misfired, and the boat had become the object of a battle of wits between Striker and himself.

In true SAS style, Striker had now taken the initiative. He had come into enemy territory, if not to kill, to tantalise. He was putting it up to the Hawk and his men. He had thrown down the gauntlet and dared them to pick it up.

Sean the Hawk gripped his Kalashnikov until his knuckles turned white. If it was action Striker wanted, he wouldn't be disappointed. He would soon learn that it wasn't through lack of daring that his adversary had come to be called the Hawk.

Working his way around the back of the meadow, he concealed himself in the ruins of an old cottage, and using his field-glasses took one last look out across the sallies. The boys were still there and there was no sign of Striker. Making a wide sweep so that he could cross the river unnoticed, he set out to see if he could locate Striker's camp. If successful, he would hit it at first light.

Chapter Nine

It had been a long day. Striker was as fresh and as fit as ever, but his men were tired and hungry. Like all soldiers on patrol, they had extra bits and pieces with them to keep them going, things like chocolate and chewing gum. However, the hunger pains reminded them that it was time they had something more substantial.

'What do you think, Sarge?' asked Smith. 'Can we have a brew up?'

Striker nodded.

'Are you sure?' asked Smith. 'It's all right to light the Hexamine?'

'Of course I'm sure. The Hawk and his men have to eat too, and they're probably planning their next move at this very moment. So why not? And get something for Peacock and Mannering while you're at it. They won't be able to brew up after dark.'

Peacock and Mannering had just begun a stint in their strategically placed observation posts. After dark these would become listening posts, and Striker had decreed that they should be manned on a two-hour rota basis.

Smith and Brown began to go through their pouches to see what they had left of their pack rations.

'What I'd love now is fish and chips,' said Brown. 'Chips not soggy but fresh and crisp, salt and vinegar, a nice bit of smoked cod, all nicely wrapped and almost too hot to handle. Do you know I can almost smell them now.'

'Well, you'd better not start smacking your chops out here,' said Smith, 'or the Hawk might decide to join you for supper.'

Striker was thinking; Smith was right. Cooking in a combat situation could be a dead giveaway. But then it might be no harm to tempt the Hawk just that little further. 'What have you got there?' he asked them.

'A jar of beef paste ... biscuits ...' Brown told him, and giving in to his desire for something more appetising continued, '... beef casserole ...'

'... and chicken curry,' added Smith hopefully.

To their surprise, Striker replied, 'Jolly good. Have whatever you fancy. You've had a hard day. Don't be long and when you've finished, relieve Mannering and Peacock so they can eat.'

As Striker crept off through the undergrowth to join Willoughby who was keeping an eye on the boys, Smith said, 'Well blow me!'

Brown nodded. 'I thought it was going to be beef paste and biscuits.'

With the typical suspicion that soldiers have of superior ranks when they don't fully understand what's going on, and they get a feeling that maybe they're being used in a way they shouldn't be used, neither of them moved to make their meal.

'What's he up to then?' wondered Brown.

Smith shook his head. 'I'd love a curry, but the Hawk would smell it a mile away ...' He stopped. 'Unless ...' He swore under his breath. 'The crafty bugger. That's what he's up to.'

'You mean he wants to let the Hawk know where we are? But that would make us sitting ducks!'

Smith took out his small Hexamine cooker. About the size of William's tobacco box, it opened out into a shallow H-shape, thus providing four legs to stand on and four uprights on which to rest a mess tin. Breaking one tablet of firelighter into four, he placed a piece in each corner so as to give an even spread of heat, and half-filled his mess tin with water. 'With our OP's in position, we're safe enough. And I don't know about you, but I'm ravenous.'

Never a one to look a gift horse in the mouth, Brown lit his cooker too and when the water was boiled, they took out their pre-cooked packets of beef casserole and chicken curry and put them into it. In less than fifteen minutes they were ready, and when they were opened a most appetising aroma was released into the evening breeze . . .

'What would you be having if you were at home now?' asked Smith.

Brown, who was leaning back on his elbow, mess tin in one hand, spoon in the other, laughed. 'I'd be having a few pints of bitter down at the local with my missus.' He swallowed a spoonful of his beef casserole and reflected, 'Tomorrow, we'd have a lie-in. We always have a lie-in on Sunday mornings . . . until the kids come in, that is. Jump all over the bed they do. Then I'd go down to the local again for a few more pints of bitter and a laugh with my mates.'

Smith smiled. 'I meant, what would you be having to eat?'

Brown wiped his mouth with the back of his hand. 'I told you. Fish and chips.'

When they had all eaten, Striker ordered them to take up a new position in heavier cover a short distance away. There Mannering and Peacock were given new observations posts, while Smith, Brown and Willoughby were told to dig in.

'I want you to dig four shell scrapes,' Striker told them. 'Here, here, here and here, each facing out like the points of a star. Make them at least eighteen inches deep and don't scrimp. They'll be our beds for the night, but if the shooting starts, they'll be our bunkers.' As they began to dig, he took several flares out of his back-pack, adding, 'I'll rig up an early warning system, and I'll expect those shell scrapes to be dug by the time I get back.'

Striker needn't have worried. Realising that his unique star-shape formation would enable them to sleep with their rifles by their side and respond instantly to trouble from any direction, they set about their task with an enthusiasm that only self-preservation could have engendered.

Striker, meanwhile, having informed his sentries what he was doing, rigged up a series of trip–flares on the outer perimeter of their position. Each flare was connected to a trip-wire in such a way that if the wire was moved, the pin would be pulled and the flare would light up the surrounding area. When Striker returned, he rehearsed the others so that they were quite clear in their minds where each was positioned, especially the sentries. The last thing he wanted was for them to start shooting at each other.

'Now, if the Hawk is going to strike,' he told them, 'he'll probably make his move just as it's getting dark, or at dawn. By now he'll have a fair idea where we are, but not precisely. This time he'll be on our side of the border, and we'll be waiting for him.'

'Strange isn't it?' said James Pius.

'What?' asked William.

'How the RUC have green uniforms and the gardai have blue.'

'What's strange about that?'

'Well, you would think it would be the other way around, wouldn't you?'

William had put a black plastic sheet, which was part of his survival equipment, on the ground under the shelter, and they were sitting on it, side by side, looking into the fire.

Thinking of the nights he would sit at the fire in his grandfather's cottage, James Pius went on, 'My grandfather believes that some day unity will come, like a rainbow spanning the border and pulling the two parts together.'

'And who's going to bring that about?' asked William. 'The IRA? After all the Protestants they've killed and maimed in the past twenty years.'

'The loyalists have killed a lot of Catholics too,' said James Pius.

'Well, we didn't start it.'

'Neither did we.' James Pius reflected for a moment. 'Anyway, the Brits were forced to leave the South in 1922 and it's only a matter of time before they're forced to leave here too.'

'But the situation's different now,' William pointed out. 'There are a million Protestants here who don't want the British to go, and who don't want anything to do with your united Ireland. What are you going to do with them?'

There was a silence, then William added, 'Anyway, they couldn't do it in 1690, and they won't do it in 1990.'

James Pius realised that William was harking back to the Battle of the Boyne again. That's what annoyed him about Protestants, he thought; they were always on about the Battle of the Boyne. He was also annoyed at William's suggestion that a Pope could have said prayers for the success of a Protestant army over a Catholic army. However, all he said was, 'I suppose you think King Billy rode a white horse?'

'Of course he did.'

James Pius laughed. 'You must be joking. It was a brown horse, a chestnut. Everybody knows that.'

Strangely enough this remark struck as sharply at William's beliefs as the remark about the Pope had struck at James Pius's. The picture of William of Orange emerging from the Boyne on his white charger, sword in hand, was the very symbol of Protestantism. It was painted on gable walls in all Protestant areas of the North; it was carefully touched up every year as the Twelfth of July approached; it adorned the Orange arches and it was a central feature of their banners.

'In Glorious Memory'. That's what it always said beneath the gold and crimson crown, and he could recall almost every detail of the colourful figure of the King on the end wall of the street where he sometimes stayed ... the flowing crimson coat lined with blue, the orange sash draped on his left shoulder and tucked in at the waist on his right side, his thigh-length riding boots, and the small golden crowns that adorned the saddle and the halter of his white horse.

'It was a white horse,' asserted William.

'How could it have been white?' said James Pius. 'Sure he would have been a sitting duck for every man with a musket.'

'Well, then, that proves he was on a white horse. Wasn't he shot in the shoulder the day before the battle, when he was reconnoitring the area?'

'You can say what you like,' said James Pius, 'it was a brown horse. Sure I saw a painting of it, done soon afterwards, which is more than you did.'

William looked at him disbelievingly. 'Where?'

'In the Bank of Ireland in Dublin.'

William grunted. 'And what would a painting of William of Orange be doing in a bank in Dublin?'

'Because the Bank of Ireland building at College Green used to be the all-Ireland Parliament. Do they not teach you anything in Protestant schools?'

James Pius thought of the day he had gone to Dublin with his father, and a friend had taken them in to see the House of Lords which the Bank of Ireland had preserved. A huge tapestry on one wall bore the words, 'The Glorious Battle of the Boyne', and showed King William, sword in hand, on his horse. However, it was a chestnut charger, and he wasn't crossing the Boyne the way he was in the pictures the Protestants painted on their walls.

The tapestry on the opposite wall, he recalled, was headed, 'The Glorious Defence of Londonderry', and showed King

James and his men surveying the besieged city. Maybe it was the way the artist had shown the sun glinting on the rump of James's horse, or maybe the tapestry was just worn; he wasn't sure, but he thought that James's horse was the one that looked white.

His father had told him that the building had housed an all-Ireland Parliament until two years after the 1798 rebellion when Britain brought in the Act of Union and abolished it. It still contained the mace of the House of Commons, the ornate metal staff that symbolised the authority of the Speaker, the man who presided over the proceedings. The last Speaker, John Foster, had refused to hand over the mace, saying it had been given to him for safe-keeping by the Irish Parliament and that he was holding on to it until another Irish Parliament returned. Some day, his father had whispered to him, there would be another all-Ireland Parliament, only this time Britain would have no hand, act or part in it.

'It seemed to me,' James Pius continued, 'that King James was the one who was riding the white horse.'

William grunted again. 'Well if he was, it didn't do him much good. We won, remember?'

James Pius cast his eyes up to heaven and said, 'Will you ever let us forget?'

Having reconnoitred the woods on the far side of the river, Sean the Hawk rejoined his men just as young Cathal was returning with food which he had collected from a sympathiser who lived in the area. As he slipped in beside them, he took a sandwich which Cathal offered him, panting, *'Go raibh míle maith agat.'*

'Aye, a thousand thanks, Cathal Óg,' repeated Seamus. 'We're all famished.'

As they ate, Sean the Hawk told them that he now had a pretty good idea where Striker and his men were located.

'I was so close to them, I could even tell what they were having for their dinner.'

'And what were they having, as a matter of interest?' asked the Professor.

'Curry. I could smell it.'

'Curry? You must hand it to the Brits,' said Seamus, 'they look after themselves.'

'We'll hand it to them all right,' retorted the Hawk. 'First thing in the morning.'

'Could we not slip across the river during the night and get the boat instead?' asked Cathal Óg.

'Not a chance,' replied the Hawk. 'With that fire going over there, Striker will be watching the boys with an image intensifier. All those things need is the light of a cigarette and they'll show you the whole area.'

'Won't he be able to slip down and get the boat then?' asked Seamus. 'The minute it gets dark.'

Sean the Hawk shook his head. 'He must assume Gadafy has given us night vision equipment as well as everything else. Anyway, it's too chancy moving about at night. For all he knows we've got the place booby-trapped.'

'But we haven't, have we?' said the Professor.

The Hawk looked at him. 'Not yet, but we soon will have. Now here's what we're going to do . . .'

Chapter Ten

William got up and walked over to the river. 'I don't know about you, but I'm hungry.'

James Pius came over to watch as he pulled in the line.

'Just one,' said William, 'and it's not very big.' He unhooked it and threw the line back into the river. 'Maybe we'll have better luck in the morning.'

James Pius picked it up. He too was feeling hungry again. 'Still, it's not bad.'

'Here, I'll clean it.' William took the fish, cut off its head and tail, and gutted it. The cleaning part was more difficult than he expected, but he managed by washing it out in the river.

'The stone's nice and warm,' James Pius called down to him. 'I'd say it's just right.'

As they sat watching the trout cooking slowly in the middle of the fire, neither spoke. For once, they didn't regard each other as a smart Alec. Instead, they appreciated the fact that they were going to get something to eat.

It was the army officer who had shown William how to catch minnow with flower petals and put a string of hooks into the river, and now as he and James Pius picked the bones of the trout, he thought of the morning and wondered what they would eat then if there wasn't another fish on the line.

'Anything that walks or crawls, swims or flies, is edible,' the officer had told him in his clipped, high-class English accent. 'Worms are 100 per cent protein. Squeeze the soil out of them, and boil them. Just like eating spaghetti. Good protein.' Then he had added. 'White maggots are good too. Taste like peanut butter.'

William reckoned he would need to be very very hungry to try anything like that. However, if all came to all, he thought he might try a frog.

'You can eat a frog,' the officer had told him, 'but not the skin. That's toxic. Stay away from rats. If you burst the spleen, jaundice.'

William knew there was no danger that he would get jaundice from a rat; there was just no way he would go near one. But, he thought again, he might try a frog. He had heard on TV that frogs' legs tasted like chicken, and he didn't find the thought of eating them too repulsive.

When they had picked the bones of the trout clean, they had a drink of water from a spring they had found nearby, built up the fire and lay down, side by side, beneath the shelter, with the *Erin go Bragh* between them. The fire, they reckoned, would keep them warm during the night; they also felt it would keep back the darkness and make them feel safer, but that was something they couldn't admit, at least not to each other.

As they lay there, listening to the crackle of the burning logs, James Pius wondered, and not for the first time, how he had come to be with a black Protestant, especially one that was named after William of Orange. William, on the other hand, was wondering how he was going to explain that he had spent a night with a Roman Catholic with the name of James Pius. Their only consolation was that between them rested the boat, and on it flew a flag to which each owed allegiance.

'Are there many in your family?' asked William after a while. He had been told that Catholics always had big families.

'There's just my sister, Martina, and myself. The others have all left home. What about you?' James Pius had always been told that Protestants had small families.

'Just me.' There was silence for a while, then William continued, 'You know, what I can't understand is how anyone can have a name like James Pius. I mean, Pius is a pope's name.'

James Pius pushed himself up on one elbow. 'And what's wrong with that?'

'Nothing, It just seems odd, that's all, being called after a pope.'

'I see nothing odd about it. I know a fella called Joseph Mary, after the parents of Christ.'

'Joseph Mary? That's a funny name for a boy.'

'I'd rather be called after the Pope or the parents of Christ than after a Dutch king who came to Ireland to fight for the British.'

William ignored the remark. Instead he was thinking of the statues of Mary and Jesus that he had seen at cross-roads and in road-side grottoes in the South. 'You have statues in your churches too. That's another thing I could never understand. How come Catholics worship statues?'

James Pius sighed deeply. The ignorance of his Protestant companion seemed to know no bounds. 'We don't worship statues,' he declared. 'They're only there as an image, a reminder that we're in God's presence.'

'The Bible says you shouldn't have images.'

'It says you shouldn't worship images, and I told you, we don't.' After another silence, James Pius added, 'But then Mary plays a more important part in our religion than she does in yours.'

'So do statues,' said William. 'And that's another thing. How come you people are always seeing statues moving? You never hear Protestants talking about moving statues or miracles.'

James Pius decided he had had enough of this talk and was no longer going to take William seriously, so he smiled to himself in the darkness and replied, 'That's because ours is the true Church.'

'It's the only Church that matters down there, as far as I can see. They even have their prayers on the television every night.'

James Pius leaned up on his elbow again. 'Why shouldn't we have the Angelus on television?'

'Why should Protestants have to listen to it? How come they don't have *their* prayers on the television?'

'They don't have to listen to ours if they don't want to,' declared James Pius. 'Anyway, the situation is reversed up here, isn't it? The Protestants are in the majority and we have to put up with it.'

William said nothing.

'*We* don't like the Twelfth of July,' James Pius continued, 'but we have to put up with that.'

'You don't have to watch it if you don't want to,' said William.

James Pius snorted. 'No, but we have to listen to it whether we want to or not. You never miss an opportunity to beat your drums and remind us who won the Battle of the Boyne.'

'The Twelfth of July's just a parade,' William protested. 'Nothing more.'

James Pius gave a derisory snigger and got up to put more wood on the fire.

As the new wood began to crackle, William thought of the bonfires that blazed across the North each year to mark the Twelfth. He would march with his father in the Orange parade, and the following day go with his Uncle Robert and the Blackmen to see the sham battle at Scarva in County Down. Both organisations were devoted to upholding the Protestant faith and maintaining the union with Britain, and at a time when the Protestant community was under so much pressure from the IRA he felt a tremendous amount of comfort in the company of such vast numbers.

To walk with the Orangemen and their bands to the 'field', there to picnic and listen to the speeches of loyalty to the Crown, was also a great day out. It was a day of billowing banners and stirring music, with the flute and fife bands playing such lilting tunes as *The Green Grassy Slopes of the Boyne, Derry's Walls,* and *Lillibulero.*

The day at Scarva was a great day out too. It was at Scarva that King William had camped on his way to the Boyne after landing at Carrickfergus, and the celebration involved a sham battle not far from an old tree where the King had tethered his horse — a white horse. After the Blackmen marched past in full regalia, it was time for another picnic and the spectacle of horsemen dressed up as William and James, their generals and troops, re-enacting some of the famous battles.

The day at Scarva also provided William with a fascinating peep into a society which, it was said, had even more secrets than the Orange Order.

Both his father and his Uncle Robert would leave their regalia with relatives or friends, rather than risk having it found in their house at the border. At the end of the Orange parade, his father would just give his sash and bowler hat to a friend, and that was that. His Uncle Robert, on the other hand, would go to the home of a third brother, Uncle John. Both Robert and John had collected an impressive array of sashes and collarettes as they progressed through the Orange Order, the Royal Arch Purple, and into the various degrees of the Royal Black Institution. Pinned to these was an even more impressive array of emblems. Among them was one depicting the lips of silence, meaning that their secrets were not to be revealed, and of all three organisations, William knew from what he had seen and heard that the Black Institution was the most senior and most secretive.

As far as he could make out, the Blackmen had secret rituals for new members, secret handshakes and secret passwords. What these were, and why they were necessary, he couldn't even guess. On occasion, he had inquired about the emblems, which they pinned to their collarettes and sashes like badges, and had been told that many of them had a Biblical meaning. Beyond that, his uncles would tell them no more; their lips were sealed.

The significance of the emblems of King William, the Crown, and the Bible, was of course obvious, but not the seven-stepped ladder, or the one consisting of a heart, cross and anchor. And certainly not the goat, or the skull and cross-bones. They always intrigued him. Equally intriguing were the Biblical scenes on the banners, and on the pictures and wall charts in Uncle John's house. The all-seeing eye, which looked down on him from the wall of one room, seemed to be watching him from whatever angle he stole a look at it, and he had no doubt it was the eye of God. Then there were the pictures of the dove returning to Noah's ark with an olive-branch in its mouth, and of the ark beneath the rainbow. Somehow as he lay and thought about them now, he couldn't imagine the dove ever bringing peace to Ireland. Nor was there any way he could envisage that rainbow spanning the border to bring both parts of the country together, the way James Pius's grandfather said it would.

James Pius sat down so that his back was to William and looked into the fire. To him and his family, the Twelfth of July was much more than just the parade William had said it was. On the contrary, as far as they were concerned, it was a day when Protestants reminded Catholics who had won the battles of the past.

'My father says *Lillibulero* was a song that mocked King James's decision to appoint a Catholic Viceroy in Ireland,' said James Pius.

'I never heard the words of it,' William replied, 'so I don't know what it means.'

'He also says it mocked the watchcry used by Catholics during their rising in 1641.'

'Huh.' William pushed himself up on his elbows. 'And you say we're the ones with the long memories!' He lay down again, adding, 'All I know is, it's a tune the bands sometimes play. And the Twelfth is just a parade. I told you that.'

James Pius said no more. According to his father, *Lillibulero* was the marching tune of King William's army at the Battle of the Boyne, and that was why the Orangemen marched to it now, three hundred years later. However, as far as his father was concerned, the battle wasn't over ...

His had been a big family, and the house had always been full, or so it had seemed to James Pius and his younger sister, Martina. From the time they had been knee-high, they had enjoyed the robust company of their big brothers and the motherly affection of their big sister. There were Gaelic games to go to on Sundays, and nights at the fire when they would hear songs and stories of the past.

Sometimes they would hear their father talking about the times before the present troubles began, times when the North had been relatively peaceful, and that was something they found very difficult to imagine. He would tell them that in those years only a handful of IRA men had continued the battle, coming mostly from the South and carrying out occasional attacks on RUC stations in places like Rosslea and Derrylin, just inside the Fermanagh border. One of the most famous, he would recall, was from his own native Limerick, Sean South of Garryowen, who was attached to a guerilla column in County Fermanagh. South, he told them, was a gifted artist, and when resting in homes sympathetic to the cause, would sketch for the children and teach them Irish. He was killed in an attack on the RUC Station at Brookeborough in 1957, but his memory lived on.

Sometimes, when friends called and their father had a whiskey or two, he would sing the ballad of Sean South:

> *The wee ones in Fermanagh homes*
> *Are asking where you've gone.*
> *Where is the red-haired soldier*
> *Who spoke our Gaelic tongue?*
> *Beside the fires he drew for us*
> *And spoke of Pearse and Tone.*
> *Ah! a mháthair, will we meet again,*
> *Sean South of Garryowen?*

They had all come to know the words well and would join him in singing the last line.

Sean South, however, was a long time ago. When the civil rights marchers came along in the late sixties, his father would tell them, the nationalist consciousness was reawakened, and then the present campaign began. Apart from the neighbours who called, there were other comings and goings, sometimes in the middle of the night, and they all knew, without being told, that their father was still actively involved in the movement. At that time, they were all fairly young, and he was the only one involved, but as they got older and the troubles continued, things changed.

Worthwhile work was scarce, and in many cases, they reckoned that with their religion and background, it would be a waste of time even to apply. Mick and Sis did succeed in getting jobs, but not the others. The IRA, however, were glad of their services, and soon even Mick and Sis had given up their jobs to devote their time to the cause. Gradually, James Pius recalled, life became more difficult. Raids on their house became more frequent and more violent, searches of their car more thorough, delays at the checkpoints longer, the abuse more vile. Each late-night rap on the door, each bend on the road, also brought the danger of loyalist assassination. However, it wasn't the loyalist paramilitaries, but the Crown forces who killed his brother Seamus.

The shooting of Seamus had been a dreadful blow to them, and with the others either in jail or on the run, James Pius was the only brother able to attend the funeral. A piper played a lament, and the emblems of Seamus's membership of the IRA, his black beret and leather gloves, rested on the Tricolour that covered the coffin. The other emblems of membership were produced later when a volley of shots was fired over his grave.

Seamus was shot dead as he sat in his car at a checkpoint. The security forces said a member's weapon had gone off accidently, but his parents didn't believe that. The inquest, when it was eventually held, didn't help to dispel their suspicion that there had been some sort of cover-up, and they were adamant that the fight to find out what exactly had happened would continue.

For both James Pius and Martina, Seamus's death was a most harrowing experience, but the imprisoning of their other two brothers, and especially their sister, was, if anything, even more heartbreaking. To see them alive, yet caged like animals, was almost more than they could bear.

Sometimes they would go with their parents to visit Sis in the women's prison at Maghaberry, or Sean and Mick in the Maze, and it was on such a journey that they first heard their mother insisting to their father that neither of them should be allowed to become involved in the movement. Whatever about himself, James Pius knew his mother had no cause to worry about Martina; she had her own ideas about the situation. Violence, she felt, had brought them nothing but trouble and the sooner it was ended the better.

However, James Pius had his ideas too, and he thought of the occasions when, after the prison visits, they went on to see relatives in Belfast and give them the latest news.

Once, he recalled, they stayed over in Belfast during the Twelfth of July, and his view of the Twelfth was very different from William's. It wasn't William of Orange, astride a white horse, sword in hand, that adorned the gable walls of the area they were in, but large pictures of the Provos in black Balaclavas, pointing the way forward with high-powered rifles and Russian rocket launchers.

Nor was it a festive occasion for the people who lived there. The security forces had erected portable screens at the end of the street, although whether these were to keep the nationalists in or the Orangemen out, he wasn't quite sure. In any event, they couldn't keep out the sound of the flute and fife bands, or the beat of the Lambeg drums, and when the other boys started throwing stones James Pius needed no encouragement to join them. However, the high screens did their work, and the Orangemen continued merrily on their way to the strains of *Lillibulero*.

James Pius lay down again, and putting a hand on the *Erin go Bragh*, said, 'We'll try the boat out tomorrow.'

William turned on his back and looked at him. 'We'll have to find a lake first.'

'Don't worry. We'll find one.'

William turned on his side and also put a hand back down to the boat, adding, 'Then I'll have to be on my way.'

James Pius didn't reply, and nothing more was said by either of them. Instead, they closed their eyes, blissfully unaware that between them lay a powerful IRA bomb, and that with every twist and turn in their sleep, they would be in danger of setting it off.

Chapter Eleven

During the night a heavy mist rose from the river, and as an early dawn began to break Sean the Hawk and his men split into pairs and stole across the river at different points.

Making their way up through the woods, the Professor and Cathal Óg kept going until they reached a by-road where itinerants had left several piebald horses to graze. By leading one, which had a rope halter on its head, and quietly coaxing the others to follow, they manoeuvred the horses across the misty fields, through a gap in a stone wall and into the woods. There they released them and by walking behind them, quietly encouraged them to move down through the woods, parallel to the river.

Stopping well short of where they reckoned Striker and his men were, the Professor and Cathal Óg checked their watches. Sean the Hawk and Seamus, they reckoned, should be in position. Taking a stick, they whacked the nearest horse on the rump, then, to make sure they kept running and to add to the confusion, fired two volleys in the air from their Kalashnikov rifles.

Almost immediately, several flares went whizzing up through the trees as the horses crashed through Striker's trip-wires. Seconds later, the flares burst above the mist and spread an eerie pink light across the woods.

In spite of the fact that they were expecting an attack, Striker's men were taken aback by the sight of several large horses careering down on top of them, and would have panicked but for the fact that Striker shouted at them to hold their ground and stay down.

It was good advice. Those in deep undergrowth breathed a sigh of relief as the horses crashed past them, while those who had been dozing in their trenches, grabbed their rifles, kept their heads down and were thankful that they had dug as deeply as Striker had told them to do.

When the horses had passed and the soldiers found themselves still in one piece, those facing the direction from which the horses had come and from which they believed the attack would now follow, opened fire, while those facing the other way turned to lend their support.

Once again, however, Striker ordered them to stay where they were and to stay down. This time it was advice that saved their lives, for no sooner had the sound of the horses' hooves died away and they had resumed their positions, than there was firing from the direction in which the horses had just gone. And unlike the first two bursts of shots, they knew these were for real.

Fortunately, because of Striker's unique star-shaped formation, those facing in that direction were able to return the fire even as the bullets sliced through the trees and undergrowth above them. In fact, they were ideally placed in their trenches to take on their attackers, and with the help of the man on sentry duty on that side of the woods, engaged their attackers in a withering cross-fire.

Within seconds, the attack died down, but even as it did, they came under attack, this time from the direction in which the horses had come. Again, thanks to Striker's star-shaped formation, some of them were well placed to respond.

Suddenly it was all over. The Hawk and his men had gone, the flares had died down and the woods were quiet.

'What do you think, Sarge?' asked Mannering. 'Did we get anything of them?'

'The blasted mist,' said Striker. 'If it hadn't been for that we'd have had them. Right. Mannering, Brown, you come with me. Those first shots were only a decoy, which means the Hawk carried out the main attack. We'll see if we can get him crossing the river. The rest of you hold your position, and don't get trigger-happy when we're coming back.'

Because of the mist and the dangers it might hold, it was some time before Striker located the two points from which Sean the Hawk and Seamus had fired on them. 'Be careful,' he warned the others. 'We don't want to walk into a booby-trap.'

Cautiously they made their way forward. 'Look here, Sarge,' whispered Mannering, 'we must have wounded one of them. There's blood on this tree.'

'Probably leaned up against it when he was hit,' said Striker.

Brown had gone down a narrow pathway ahead of them. 'And here's a live round,' he called back to them. 'He must have dropped it.'

Seeing him bending down to pick it up, Striker cried, 'No! No!' But it was too late.

For one terrifying moment, they saw Brown's dis-integrating body framed in a blinding flash. In the same instant, they were blown off their feet and hurled across the ground. Rolling over, they covered the backs of their heads with their hands, as all around them trees and branches came crashing down, and a shower of stones, soil and other debris pelted their prostrate bodies.

When the drumming on their backs had stopped, an eerie silence descended on the woods.

Spotting his rifle nearby, Striker reached out to retrieve it and squirmed around so that he was in a position to respond to any further attacks. However, none came, and he eased himself up. 'Bastards,' he muttered, and seeing Mannering coming to life inquired, 'Are you all right?'

Dazed and trembling, and hardly able to believe he was

still in one piece, Mannering nodded.

'Right. Back to the others.'

'But what about Brown?' asked Mannering.

'What about him? He's dead! Now get a move on. I'll cover you.'

The shock which Brown's death caused to the other members of the patrol, was eclipsed only by Striker's decision to leave the body, or what was left of it, where it was.

'It's not right, Sarge,' Smith protested when Striker had finished talking to the OC on the radio. 'Brown was one of our mates.'

Striker sighed, and thought what wouldn't he give for one or two of his own mates just now, hardened soldiers like himself. Even one would do.

'We can't move him until we check out that whole area for booby-traps,' he told them, 'and we're not going to do that — not yet.'

'You mean, not until the mist clears,' said Peacock.

'I mean, not until it suits us,' said Striker. 'The minute we bring in a helicopter, the Hawk and his men will know they've scored a hit, and I don't intend giving them that satisfaction. It might also make them do something daft, like blowing up the boat and maybe the boys with it.' He paused as if weighing up the possibilities. 'As it is, we've wounded two of them ... one down at the lake, and one up here this morning. That puts us in a good position to even the score.'

Smith couldn't help thinking that Striker seemed to regard the whole thing as some sort of game. The words of another sergeant were also going through his head, the one who had seen them off at the base. 'We don't want to give some trigger-happy Paddy a good aiming mark,' he had barked at Willoughby. 'Your mother wouldn't like that, would she?' Brown's mother wouldn't like it either, Smith thought. Or his wife. No more pints of bitter in his local, no more laughs with his mates, no more lying-on with his wife on Sunday mornings, no more romping around the bed with his kids. A few lines in the papers, a flash on the telly ... that would be all. Brown was now just another statistic.

'The Hawk's clever all the same,' Mannering was saying.

Striker shook his head. 'It wasn't the Hawk's cleverness that killed Brown. It was Brown's stupidity.' The hard edge of what he was saying cut through the numbness in their minds like a knife, just as he intended it should do. 'How many times have you been told not to pick things up? A bullet, a girlie magazine ... PIRA will make a booby-trap out of anything like that. A nylon thread attached to the underside of it, and you trigger the bomb right under your own feet. How many times have you been warned?'

They nodded, but said nothing. Brown's death had brought home to them in the most cruel and shattering way, the harsh reality of soldiering in Northern Ireland. Now as Striker continued to berate them, they realised how easy it would be for them to make the same mistake. They also realised, in spite of Striker's confidence, just how difficult it was going to be to get the Hawk.

William and James Pius had spent a restless night beneath their makeshift shelter, but differ as they might about religion, the same God must have watched over them and somehow the plastic starfish that had trembled and flickered inside the boat had failed to make contact.

When the fire had died down, the night had become cold. William's ex-army clothes, however, were designed for just such a situation, and in addition he had taken the precaution of bringing an extra tee-shirt with him.

'The more thin layers of clothing you have, the more air you trap,' the officer had told him, 'and that means the more insulated you are against the cold. A woollen jumper will trap the air too, but the extra layers are better.'

98

William had taken his advice, but James Pius's jacket was light, and when the embers had grown cold, so had he. His twisting and turning had made William restless too, and neither had slept very well.

Sub-consciously, also, images of shooting, ships, flags and fish had come together in their jumbled thoughts, and at times it had seemed that the *Erin go Bragh* was sailing right up through their slumbers, dividing them in the hours of darkness as it had done during the day.

Consequently, when Cathal Óg and the Professor fired their first shots, the two boys sat up with a start, not knowing if what they had heard was real or if it had been part of their dreams.

When, moments later, the flares burst above the woods and cast their ghostly pink glow across the mist, they still weren't sure if they were dreaming. The mist was swirling all around them, shimmering with the light of the flares as they drifted slowly to the ground, and it was only when the shooting erupted in earnest that they realised a battle was in progress nearby.

'This is like Guy Fawkes' night!' gasped William. 'I thought they'd all gone away.'

They were both kneeling beside the blackened embers of the fire, instinctively keeping their heads down as they listened to the shooting.

'Only those aren't squibs.' James Pius pulled his jacket around himself as he peered through the mist.

William nodded. 'I never heard so much shooting in my life.'

James Pius lifted the *Erin go Bragh* and tucked it under his arm. 'It sounds very close.'

Just then the flares burned out, leaving the mist colourless and cold. James Pius shivered. 'I think we should move on.'

'We'll have to be careful how we go,' said William, 'but you're right. It does sound very close.'

James Pius looked at him and asked pointedly, 'Where's the control box?'

William tapped his jacket pocket, and without batting an eyelid said, 'I have it.'

Having checked to make sure they were leaving nothing behind, the two of them said no more but quietly stole away through the mist.

Though it was a heavy mist, they found they could see for several yards all around, and were thus able to make their way slowly along the river bank without danger of falling in.

After some time, however, the river opened out into a lake, and they found the going much more difficult. At first they reckoned that if they kept to the shoreline, they would eventually make their way past it, but when the stony shore gave way to soggy ground and the familiar tall stalks of reeds, the situation changed.

They stopped and listened. The shooting had died down and the lake was silent and still. Even the reeds, which forever seemed to be rustling, were quiet, their seed heads bowed beneath the glistening droplets of mist. For a moment the ghostly white figures of two swans glided into view, moving so gracefully it seemed they were propelled by something other than webbed feet, and then they were gone, disappearing into the mist just as quietly as they had come.

Realising that as they had paused, almost transfixed by the silence of the lake, the water had begun to creep up around their feet, they turned away in search of firmer ground. Just then a huge explosion ripped down along the river, reverberating like thunder as it echoed and re-echoed across the mist and into the distance beyond. Instinctively they stopped and ducked, not knowing it was the booby-trap bomb that had gone up, thinking it was like an artillery shell whizzing over their heads.

Nearby there was a plop, then the flitter of wings across the surface of the water, as a rat and a coot, not wishing to reveal themselves but frightened by the noise, were prompted into an involuntary movement that betrayed their presence beneath the all-enveloping mist.

Whatever effect the explosion had on the wildlife, it gave James Pius such a fright that he almost dropped the boat.

'I wonder what's going on?' whispered William.

Looking up around him as if expecting to see something coming crashing down on them, James Pius clutched the boat even tighter and replied, 'Search me.' He withdrew his feet from the soggy ground and, stepping lightly, continued his way gingerly along the lake shore.

William pulled the collar of his jacket up around his neck, took a firm hold of the control box and followed him.

By now, the mist had settled on their heads and shoulders, giving them an odd grey-like appearance, and they could feel it cold on their hands and on their face. It was still very early in the morning and they wondered when the mist would lift.

'I don't ever remember such a heavy mist at this time of year,' said William.

James Pius stopped and looked around him again. 'If you lived where I do, you'd see it often enough. It's all these lakes and the wet ground.' He walked on, his feet squelching as if to underline what he was saying. 'Some of the land in this part of the country is so bad Cromwell didn't even think it was worth giving away. It was good enough for the Irish, of course. Anything would do them.' When William ignored him, he added, 'Anyway, it'll probably lift before long.'

A few moments later, they found themselves at the water's edge again, so they turned to their left where they imagined firmer ground was to be found. However, again they came to the same soft, squelching shoreline as before, and soon it seemed that no matter which way they turned, they were walking into the lake.

'We're going round in circles,' said William at last. The

officer who had talked to him about survival hadn't mentioned anything about crossing treacherous terrain in a mist. Had he done so, his advice would probably have been to stay put until the mist cleared, but with all the shooting that was going on that hadn't been possible.

Pausing for a moment, William reached into the pocket of his combat jacket and took out his survival box. At least, he thought as he untaped the lid, his button compass might enable them to walk away from the lake in a straight line, although where that line would lead them to he had no idea.

'What are you looking for in there now?' inquired James Pius. 'A rubber dingy?'

'Very funny.' William continued to poke through the contents of his tobacco tin with his forefinger. Then he looked at James Pius accusingly, and demanded, 'All right, where is it?'

James Pius looked back at him with a face that was the picture of innocence. 'Where's what?'

'You know well what — the compass. Come on, where is it?'

'I don't know what you're talking about.'

William held the box out towards him, saying, 'It was in there last night, and it's not there now.'

'So, what are you looking at me for? If you put it back in the box, it should be there still. Unless, of course, you dropped it on the grass.'

William taped the lid back on and put the box in his jacket pocket. Of all the things in the box the compass was one of the most important, and he had taken great care to put it back. James Pius, he was certain, had taken it, probably when he had gone to set the rabbit snare. Indeed, now that he thought about it, he had been suspicious of James Pius's readiness on that occasion to agree not to interfere with the Union Jack. But why take the compass of all things? Unless he just wanted to get his own back on him for putting the

102

flag on the boat in the first place. Either that or he was playing for time. That was probably it all right, he thought, playing for time, waiting for an opportunity to slip off with the boat.

Determined not to give James Pius the satisfaction of seeing his frustration, William looked at his watch and said, 'Anyway, I can manage without it?'

'How?'

'I can find my direction by using my watch.'

James Pius looked worried for a moment, then to disguise his concern, he guffawed and said, 'Don't tell me you have a compass in there too?'

William pushed up his sleeve a bit farther. 'No. All I have to do is point the hour hand at the sun, and by dividing the angle between the hour hand and twelve o'clock, I can find due south.'

This was something James Pius hadn't counted on when he had taken the compass, and while he realised it wouldn't work now, in the mist, he feared that it might enable William to make off with the boat when the sun came out. That meant he would have to try and get away with the boat himself before the mist lifted. In the meantime, all he could do was resort to ridicule.

Shifting the boat so that it sat more comfortably in the crook of his arm, he said, 'Go on then, show me, where's the south?'

'I told you. You need the sun.'

James Pius turned to go. 'Huh, you might as well have a digital for all the good it'll do you in this mist. And what are you going to point it at if it's cloudy?'

William said nothing for he knew James Pius was right. That was another thing the officer had forgotten to tell him. However, he had told him another way to find his direction when it was cloudy, and if, when the mist cleared, there was no sun, he would fall back on that.

'What time is it anyway?' asked James Pius.

'It's still very early,' was all William told him. 'Too early for your wisecracks.'

James Pius chuckled and kept going.

If James Pius thought his own sense of direction would lead them to safety, he was soon to find that it wasn't as simple as that. After a further period of trial and error it became obvious to him too that they had got themselves into an area where the soft, sometimes swampy, shoreline of the lake was contorted to such an extent that even William's compass, which he had concealed in the pocket of his jeans, wouldn't be sufficient to get them out of their predicament. It was, therefore, with a great sense of relief that he eventually found his feet on firm ground. 'Listen,' he said. 'There's a car. We must be near a road.'

They were standing on a low hump of land that jutted out into the lake, and on hearing the car, both jumped up on to a lump of grey-black rock that stuck up through the long lush grass.

For a moment the mist pulled apart to reveal the roadway on the other side of a narrow neck of water, but even as the car came along, the mist closed in again, and they knew that, whatever about their cries for help, their waving had been in vain.

James Pius sat down, and leaning the *Erin go Bragh* against the rock, proceeded to take off his runners.

'What are you doing?' asked William.

'It's only a few yards across. I'm going to try and wade over.'

'But you don't know how deep it is. You could get drowned.'

James Pius hung his runners around his neck, and picking up the boat, said, 'Well, if you're too chicken to go, I'm going on my own.'

'I'm not chicken,' William retorted, 'but I'm not an eejit

104

either.' He took off his jacket, and placed the survival box and the control box on the ground for safe keeping. Then he took hold of one sleeve and gave the other to James Pius, saying, 'Here, hang on to that until you see how deep it is.'

With the boat tucked firmly under one arm, and holding on to the sleeve of the coat with his other hand, James Pius ventured into the water. It was cold and the stony bottom hurt his feet, but he wouldn't please William by saying so. Wading in slowly, he felt the water creeping up until it was over his knees, then his thighs, and he hoped it would soon level out.

'Careful,' warned William, but he had scarcely spoken when James Pius went straight down, and disappeared under the water, leaving the *Erin go Bragh* rocking violently back and forth on the ripples that he left behind.

Chapter Twelve

Because Sean the Hawk and his men knew the terrain so well, the mist had worked to their advantage in launching the attack on Striker. In the same way, it had covered their retreat across the border, and they had just reached their camp when they heard the booby-trap bomb going off.

They turned to listen as the explosion reverberated down the river, and Cathal Óg wondered if it was Striker himself or one of his men who had taken the bait and picked up the bullet which the Professor had rigged up the previous night.

Sean the Hawk set his Kalashnikov down against a rock and looking up into the mist shook his head, saying, 'It's hard to know. Striker's smart, very smart.'

Seamus was sitting on another rock as the Professor, his own left hand still bandaged, cleaned a wound on the upper part of his right arm. 'If we did get any of them,' said Seamus, 'we'll soon hear the choppers coming in to take them out.'

The Hawk came over to look at Seamus's arm. 'If they can come in, in that mist . . . How is it?'

'Just a flesh wound,' said Seamus.

'Still, it's fairly deep,' said the Professor. 'I think we should get a doctor to have a look at it.'

'And what about you?'

'I'm all right. But this is going to have to be looked after.'

Sean the Hawk looked at the two of them and cursed

Striker for the umpteenth time. 'He's a good shot too. Either that or he's got a marksman.'

'You can say that again,' said Seamus. 'They were slinging lead at us from all directions, and some of it was very close.' He held up his elbow to look at the crimson stain that was spreading across the bandage, and added, 'Too close.'

'Do you think we got any of them?' asked Cathal Óg. 'I mean, apart from the booby-trap?'

Again the Hawk shook his head. 'There's no way of telling. They were well dug in.'

'I'd say they got a helluva fright when the horses came charging in on them,' laughed Cathal Óg.

In spite of the pain in his arm, Seamus managed a smile. 'It was like the Wild West there for a minute.'

'Only they've got Wyatt Earp.' The Hawk wasn't smiling when he said this, and the Professor asked him what he was going to do.

The Hawk walked around for a few moments, and the others could see that his face was dark with anger and frustration. Then turning to the Professor, he asked, 'Those 60 millimetre mortars. Do we have any stashed away in this area?'

The Professor nodded. 'There are some of them buried on Mickey Joe's farm. But you'd want to get clearance before you start digging those up.'

'You leave that to me. Would they reach Striker's position?'

'If he's still in the woods above the river, no problem.'

'All right.' He took his field-glasses from around his neck and handed them to Cathal Óg. 'You and the Professor take up position in the ruins of that old cottage, the one beyond the woods, overlooking the sallies. You can keep the boys under observation from there, and don't let them out of your sight, whatever you do.'

'And what are you going to do?' asked the Professor.

'I'll take Seamus to somebody who can look after that arm, and get some food.'

'How are you going to manage the mortars? They're fairly heavy.'

Sean the Hawk picked up his Kalashnikov and helped Seamus pull on his jacket. 'Mickey Joe has a tractor, hasn't he?' When the Professor nodded, he added, 'Well then, he can bring them. We won't be long.'

A short time later Cathal Óg and the Professor were sitting on the earthen floor of the old cottage, waiting for the mist to clear. They felt wet and hungry now and hoped the others wouldn't be too long in bringing them some breakfast. The roof of the cottage had long since gone, and a canopy of briars that had grown in over the ruins of the side walls did nothing to keep out the cold.

Cathal Óg leaned back against the gable wall, and stretched his legs straight out in front of him. 'What mortars is he going to get?'

The Professor was wiping the mist from his glasses. 'The small ones.'

Cathal nodded. He reckoned it would be the smaller ones all right, not the big ones they sometimes fired from the back of lorries. He picked up his rifle, and pressing the small lever in front of the trigger guard with his left thumb, withdrew the curved magazine, checked it, then locked it back into position again.

'All the same, the Kalashnikov has a powerful punch, hasn't it?'

The Professor put his glasses back on. 'Old Mikhail knew what he was doing all right.'

'Who?'

'Mikhail Kalashnikov, the Russian who designed it.'

'Oh.' Cathal Óg was silent for a moment. 'How's the hand?'

'It's okay, really. And so's the leg.'

'Sean didn't give you much sympathy.'

'He's just sore because he thinks I was responsible for losing the boat. I suppose he has to blame somebody.'

'What if it does blow up, do you think he'll really . . . ?'

'You mean kill me?' The Professor looked at him. 'He's capable of it all right, but I don't think so. I'm too valuable to the movement alive, and he knows it. Anyway, he'd only be putting his own neck on the line.'

'And what do you think are the chances of us getting the boat back?'

The Professor shook his head. 'I've no idea. Even if the mortars do the job and we get rid of Striker, who knows when the boat's going to go up and the boys with it?'

'And what are the chances of that happening?'

'Well, when they get to the lake, all they have to do is get it going . . . and once they start fiddling with the controls, that's it.'

Cathal Óg placed his rifle on the ground again. 'You know, I can't help feeling Sean's more interested in getting that SAS man than the boat.'

'True. But then if he gets Striker, the way would be clear to get the boat.'

In a new location in the woods on the far side of the river, a similar conversation was taking place between Willoughby and Mannering.

In spite of the mist and the danger of booby-traps, Striker had gone off on his own again, although where he went or what he did on these forays into the woods, the others could only guess.

'They certainly know what they're doing,' said Mannering.

'Who?'

'These SAS chaps. Striker could see Brown was going to get killed. He knew that bullet was a booby-trap. He tried to warn him.'

'Poor bastard,' said Willoughby.

Mannering nodded. 'And then there was that shot Smith took at the Hawk. Striker could tell straight off he was out of range, and Smith's a marksman.'

'I wonder if it's the Hawk that's wounded.'

'Impossible to say, but I hope it is — for Brown's sake.'

'You know,' said Willoughby, 'I sometimes think Striker's just using that boat as bait.'

'Well, I hope the Hawk takes it. What I wouldn't give to get him in my sights — just once.'

Willoughby nodded. 'Me too, but you know, if PIRA have come up with something new in the line of explosives, it would be very important to us to find out what it is.'

'That's true,' said Mannering. 'It might keep a few more of us from ending up like Brown.'

'Alpha 39 to base.' Willoughby adjusted his radio, and added, 'Then again, maybe Striker figures he can kill two birds with one stone!'

Fortunately for James Pius, he was holding on to the sleeve of William's jacket when he stepped into deep water. For a moment, William thought he too was going to be dragged in, but he held on and was relieved to see James Pius bobbing to the surface. Even though James Pius was coughing and spluttering, he had the presence of mind to reach out and catch the *Erin go Bragh* before it could drift away, and digging in his heels, William pulled them both into shallow water.

Still holding the boat, James Pius sat down on the rocky shore, and coughed until he had cleared the water from his lungs. The mist was still swirling in around them, and as he began to shiver, William helped him to his feet, saying, 'Come on, let's get some shelter before you freeze to death.'

William had been reluctant to go into the water, not because he was chicken, as James Pius had put it, but because he didn't like the look of it at that particular point. He had also been warned that if he ever got lost, to try and avoid getting his clothes wet unless the sun was warm enough to dry them.

'If your clothes get wet,' the army officer had told him, 'you lose body heat drying them out. You lose energy and the need for food is greater.' That, he knew, was the military way of saying that if you got wet, you could get cold and hungry very quickly.

Whatever the day might bring, the morning mist was as cold as ever, and James Pius was beginning to shiver uncontrollably.

'Here, sit down behind this rock,' said William. 'You'll have to get dried out.'

William put the control box down and reached out to take the *Erin go Bragh* which James Pius was still clutching under his arm. James Pius's teeth were chattering with the cold, but he held on to the boat, saying, 'What do you think you're doing?'

'I'm trying to get you to put the boat down so you can use your arms to work up a bit of heat.'

James Pius put the boat down himself. 'And what are you going to do?'

'I'm going to try and light a fire.'

James Pius started to flail himself with his arms, and as William disappeared into the mist, he wondered how, short of coming to blows, he was ever going to get the *Erin go Bragh* for himself.

A short time later William returned. In one hand he was carrying some dry twigs and rotten branches which he had collected from underneath some gorse bushes. With the other he was pulling more substantial pieces of gorse which he had tied together with string. If he could get these to flare up, he reckoned it might give James Pius the immediate heat he needed, and perhaps attract the attention of someone passing

111

along the nearby roadway.

Quickly he arranged the smallest and driest twigs over the piece of greasy paper that James Pius's sandwiches had been wrapped in, and then searched in his survival box for a piece of cottonwool to use as tinder. Somehow his matches had got damp, so he took out his flint and steel and showered the cottonwool with sparks. James Pius's teeth were still chattering as he watched and waited for the flame that might signal an end to his misery.

Nothing happened, so William struck the flint again. This time the cottonwool began to smoulder, and putting his face down close to it, he blew gently until a small flame appeared. Slowly the flame spread up through the greasy paper, the twigs began to crackle, and then it surged up through the branches of brittle gorse. Feeling the sudden blast of heat, James Pius was for once grateful for the magic box he had derided so often. William immediately heaped on the remainder of the branches he had brought and dashed off to get some more. When he returned, he built the fire up again, and handing James Pius his spare tee-shirt and his jacket, said, 'Here, put these on.'

James Pius murmured his thanks and having pulled on the tee-shirt, draped the jacket around his shoulders.

Crouching close to the fire to keep himself warm, William said, 'Put it on properly. It'll give you more heat.'

Again James Pius did as he was told, but as he put his hands in the pockets he felt something cold squirming around in one of them. 'What's that?' he exclaimed, jumping to his feet and holding out his hands.

William laughed, and going over to him took a large frog out of the pocket. 'Sorry. I forgot about him.'

Feeling somewhat embarrassed by the fright he had got, James Pius sat down at the fire again. 'What are you doing with that in your pocket?'

William set the frog down in the hollow between himself

and the rock where it couldn't get away. 'I picked it up on the way round the lake.'

'What for?'

'If we don't get something to eat soon, we might be glad of it.'

'What?' exclaimed James Pius. 'Eat a frog? You are mad.'

'Why, what's wrong with a frog? The French eat frogs' legs all the time.'

William turned to check that the frog was still in the hollow behind him, when above the rock he saw a strange hairy face peering down through the mist. It wasn't a bearded face, but a ruddy face with long gingery locks that grew right down to the mouth and formed a moustache. Before he could get over his surprise, the moustached mouth opened and asked in a gruff, gravelly voice, 'What do you think you're doing?'

Startled, James Pius turned around to see the large figure of a man rise above them, and look down at them through the mist.

'We're lost,' William replied.

'And I fell into the lake,' said James Pius. 'I thought I could get across to the road.'

The stranger came down to them, and they could see that in spite of the cold mist the neck of his shirt and his jacket were open. Taking a flat bottle of whiskey out of one of the sagging pockets of his jacket, he offered it to James Pius, saying, 'Here, this'll warm you.'

James Pius thanked him, but declined. He was on the verge of explaining that he had taken the pledge not to drink alcohol before he was eighteen, but thought better of it, as he knew that would reveal he was a Catholic. Somehow this strange hairy face, with its distinct military look, gave him the feeling that he might be looking at a Protestant of a different colour!

Chapter Thirteen

The reservations which James Pius had about the stranger were based on the belief which he, and indeed many others in the North had, that they could tell whether a man was a Catholic or Protestant just by looking at him.

The stranger's overgrown locks, joining as they did an equally overgrown moustache, gave him not only a military look but a rather pompous appearance, and this had led James Pius to believe that here was a man whose roots might not lie in the Orange Order or the Royal Black Institution, but in the service of the Empire. A man, perhaps, who had come from landed stock and had soldiered under the British flag in many a foreign campaign.

William had formed roughly the same opinion of the man, but to his way of thinking such a background was a recommendation in itself, and so when the man turned and walked away from the lake, he followed. Being wet and hungry, James Pius felt he had no option but to go too, and despite his reservations fell in behind them.

'So what if he was in the British army?' asked William, when James Pius gave an indication of what he was thinking. 'He's not going to bite you. And he's bound to have a house around here somewhere, maybe one of those big houses with a huge roaring fire where you can dry yourself out.'

Now and then the man vanished into the mist ahead of them, walking as if he was unaware that they were following. After one of these temporary disappearances they came upon him as he pulled a bicycle out of the undergrowth. It was only then they noticed that the legs of his trousers were tucked into his socks. Pausing only to take a swig from his bottle of whiskey, he threw his leg over the saddle, and without a word cycled unsteadily across the misty field ahead of them.

Not quite knowing what to think now, they quickened their step and kept him in sight until he dismounted and disappeared into an old caravan.

It was the most dilapidated caravan they had ever seen. Instead of having wheels, it was sitting on concrete blocks, and it was tied down with ropes as if the owner was afraid it would be blown away.

'So much for the big house,' said William.

James Pius nodded. 'I should have known. Sure who'd build a big house on land like this? Cromwell couldn't even give it away.'

'I know,' said William, 'you told me before.'

As they paused, wondering what to do, James Pius rubbed his hands together and shivered. 'It can't be any worse than standing out here.' He sniffed. 'And what's that sweet smell? I wonder if it's food?'

William was also aware of the smell. It was sweet all right, although quite different from the smell that came from his survival box. Furthermore, it was emanating from the caravan.

'Smells like food all right,' said William. 'Come on, let's go in.'

The man had lit an old paraffin heater and they were grateful for the little bit of warmth that it was already beginning to give. Despite the fumes, they could still get the sweet smell. However, as they stood with their backs to the heater and looked around, they could see that the caravan was in an unbelieveable state of filth. A disassembled fishing-rod and net lay in a tangle in one corner. Empty beer cans,

115

whiskey bottles and pieces of paper were strewn around the floor, while a mangy black cat stood on the folding table, licking the inside of a small tin which it had already licked clean.

Closing the door, the man sat down at the table, dislodging the cat and the tin with a sweep of his arm, and took the bottle of whiskey from his jacket pocket.

James Pius slid in opposite him, and resting the *Erin go Bragh* on the table said, 'I don't suppose you've anything to eat? We're starving.'

'Eat? Eat?' The man unscrewed the top of the bottle, and after drinking from it told him, 'This is all the food I need. Here, have a drop.'

'I . . . I don't drink,' said James Pius.

The man wiped his mouth and ginger moustache with the back of his hand, and burped loudly. They could now see he was very thin on top, and for the first time James Pius wondered if the real reason he had grown such enormous locks was to give the impression that he had more hair than he actually had.

The sweet smell was stronger than ever now, and seeing James Pius sniffing it, the man reached in under the table. Pulling out a plastic bucket he mumbled, 'Here, have some breadcrumbs.'

Both James Pius and William recoiled at what they saw, for the bucket was half full of crushed breadcrumbs and crawling red maggots.

Seeing the revulsion in their faces, the man guffawed loudly and after taking another drink of whiskey, told them, 'Go on, the fish love it.' He dug his hand into the crawling mess and let the breadcrumbs and maggots fall back into the bucket through his fingers. Then, addressing the maggots, he added, 'Roach and bream wouldn't say no to you, would they?'

It was then the two of them realised that what they were

looking at was the bait used on the lakes for coarse fishing.

Once again William thought of what the officer had told him about finding food. He had been talking about worms being 100 per cent protein. 'White maggots also,' he had said in his clipped upper-class English accent. 'They taste like peanut butter.' William wondered if red maggots also tasted like peanut butter. In fact, he wondered what peanut butter tasted like. However, he wasn't about to try the maggots to find out. He reckoned he would die of hunger first.

The man with the moustache now leaned forward, and resting his chin on his hands as they clutched the half-empty whiskey bottle, gazed long and low at the *Erin go Bragh*. His eyes, they could see, were going lazily back and forth from the Tricolour to the Union Jack.

'We've got to be going now,' said William.

'What's your hurry?' The man held out his arm and blocked the way to the door. 'Sit down. Sit down and have a drink.'

Reluctantly, William slid in beside James Pius and together they watched their strange host across the deck of the *Erin go Bragh*.

'We really have to be going,' repeated William.

'Not before you sing a song!' The man took another drink of whiskey, and when he leaned forward again his eyes settled on the Union Jack. 'Now, who's going to sing *The Sash*?'

William and James Pius looked at each other, convinced that the man was trying to find out which of them was the Protestant and which was the Catholic. The problem was, that, having misjudged his background, they weren't sure now what he was, and until they knew they couldn't let him know what they were. This was the unspoken message that flashed between them, and so they both began to sing :

> *It was old but it was beautiful,*
> *And its colours they were fine . . .*

117

That was the only line James Pius knew, but he went on, *Da-da da da da da da da-da*, as William filled in the words:

> *It was worn at Derry, Aughrim,*
> *Enniskillen and the Boyne,*
> *My father wore it as a youth*
> *In the bygone days of yore,*
> *And on the Twelfth I love to wear*
> *The sash my father wore.*

James Pius joined in with ... *the sash my father wore*, and hoped the man hadn't noticed that he didn't know the words.

However, the man's eyes were now on the Tricolour, and he asked, 'Now, who's going to sing *The Wearing of the Green?*'

They looked at each other again, convinced more than ever now that their host was trying to find out what religion each of them was.

William didn't know the beginning of the song, but he mumbled it as James Pius began:

> *O Paddy dear, and did you hear*
> *The news that's going round?*
> *The shamrock is by law forbid*
> *To grow on Irish ground ...*

James Pius didn't know it all either, so he skipped a few lines:

> *She's the most distressful country*
> *That ever yet was seen ...*

Even William knew the next line, and so they ended with a lusty rendering of:

> *For they're hanging men and women*
> *For the wearing of the green ...*

James Pius looked at William as if to say, 'You would

know that line, wouldn't you?' but quickly looked across the table as he felt the man place his hand on the *Erin go Bragh*.

'That's a lovely boat,' he was saying. 'You'll leave that with me.'

'It's not our boat,' James Pius protested.

'That's right,' said William, 'It belongs to someone else. We're just minding it for him.'

However, they could see the man was very drunk now, and nothing they said seemed to register with him. They thought of making a run for it, but he was sitting between them and the door, and they feared that if he caught them he might turn violent. In any case, they weren't prepared to go without the boat.

As they sat back to consider their predicament, William put his hands into his jacket. In one pocket was the control box, in the other the frog. The frog, he could feel, was sitting hunched up, probably pondering its predicament too.

'Think of something,' whispered James Pius out of the side of his mouth.

Even though the man was in a drunken stupor, he looked up when James Pius spoke, and opening his bleary eyes, said, 'What? What's that you say?'

'A . . . mmm . . . nothing,' James Pius assured him.

The man grunted and his head sagged again, but his hand remained on the deck of the boat.

The frog was now beginning to squirm beneath William's hand, and as it did so he thought of stories he had heard about men being so drunk they sometimes saw snakes crawling up walls. He didn't know if that was true, but it gave him an idea. Taking the frog from his pocket, he placed it gently on the cabin of the boat, and holding it there with one hand, tapped the man on the shoulder with the other.

'Ah, excuse me.' The man lifted his head. 'Excuse me.'

Slowly the man opened his eyes, and for a moment stared, transfixed, into the eyes of the frog. Then, thinking that he

119

was seeing things, and perhaps fearing that the drink was causing him to have hallucinations, he jerked his head back. At the same time, William released the frog, which, finding itself free for the first time in a long while, leapt straight on to the man's hairy face. With a scream of terror, he fell back on to the floor, and seizing their opportunity William and James Pius grabbed the boat and the frog and fled from the caravan.

When they stopped running, they found they were on a muddy track, but where it led to they had no idea, for the mist was still swirling around them.

'That's the last time I'm going off with anybody I don't know,' panted James Pius.

'Well, I'm sure your mother told you not to go with strangers.'

'It was you that followed him. I was only following you because I was wet.' James Pius felt his trousers. 'And after all that I'm still wet.'

William took the frog from his pocket, and stroked the back of its head. 'Did you see the look on his face when he saw it?'

James Pius managed a smile and nodded, but then as they walked on he added, 'I suppose you're going to eat it now?'

William didn't answer. Instead, he put the frog back in his pocket, saying, 'We're going to have to eat something. And you're going to get cold again if you don't get dried out.' He looked at his watch and then up at the mist. 'We're going to end up going round in circles again.'

James Pius fingered the small button compass in his pocket. 'I thought you said you could tell by your watch which way to go?'

'Ha ha, very funny.' William stopped. He was thinking of something else the officer had said when telling him how to find direction.

'Find a church,' the officer had told him. 'One of the older ones. They were often built in the form of a Cross, with the top of the Cross facing east, towards Jerusalem.'

William had since wondered if that was right, but even if it was he didn't know how it might help him to find his way in the mist.

'A church?' James Pius laughed, then added, 'Aye, it might help you to find your way all right ... if it's one of ours. Ours is the true Church, I told you that before.'

'I'm glad you think so,' William retorted. 'Anyway, I wouldn't go near one of yours.' It had now occurred to him that the officer's advice might mean having to look for a Catholic church, and he had no intention of doing that, for apart altogether from priests and statues, Mass was something his religion didn't agree with. He therefore regarded Catholic churches with great suspicion.

The argument would have continued had they not at that moment seen a small, church-like building loom up out of the mist before them. Its tiny arched windows had diamond shaped panes, and its slated roof rose at a very sharp angle. As they looked up at it, however, they could see that its quaintly shaped chimney was smoking.

'A fire!' said James Pius, and walking up to the door, which was arched in the same style as the windows, knocked loudly, his encounter with the hairy-faced man in the caravan already forgotten.

William was still looking up, trying to figure out what sort of building it was, when the door opened and a very thin, frail man appeared.

'I fell into the lake,' said James Pius.

'We lost our way,' added William by way of explanation.

'Well come in, come in,' said the man, stepping back to allow them past.

Whatever the building might have been, they could see it was now used as a house and it was in darkness, except for the glow of the fire in an old-fashioned black stove at the far end of the room.

The man motioned with his right hand, saying, 'Go on, go on. Go up and warm yourself.'

They needed no second bidding, and as the old man eased himself down into an armchair that was worn and shiny with age, they warmed their hands and then their backsides at the fire.

Sensing that this man posed no threat to them, they had no reservation about introducing themselves, and when they had done so, James Pius asked him, 'How come you've such a nice fire going so early in the morning?'

'Insomnia. I can't sleep.'

By the light of the fire they could now see that the man's face, like his body, was very thin, and his eyes were rimmed with red from lack of sleep.

There was silence and soon the steam began to rise from the back of James Pius's trousers.

The man leaned forward. 'That's a nice boat you have there.'

James Pius nodded and approached him so that he could have a closer look at it.

'This is the control box,' said William, taking it from his pocket and holding it out.

'Very nice.' The man reached up and James Pius allowed him to take the boat and hold it on his knees. 'And I see you've two flags on it.'

'Mine's the Union Jack,' said William.

James Pius hesitated for just a moment. 'Mine's the Tricolour.'

He glanced up at them. 'One of each?'

They nodded.

'You know,' he said, confirming their feeling that he was also talking about religion, 'this is a great country for flags and religion. But I can never understand people fighting about religion.' He leaned back in his chair, and still holding the boat on his knees, continued, 'When I go to meet my Maker, and I know it won't be long now, I'm certain He's not going to ask me what religion I was. He's going to want to know if I led a good Christian life. He's going to ask me *what* I did, not *how* I did it.'

'We met a man with long side-locks,' said James Pius, 'and I think he was trying to find out what we were.'

'But we didn't tell him,' said William. 'We didn't know what he was.'

'You mean George?' The old man laughed. 'Poor George. I wouldn't say he knows himself what he is. He's an alcoholic.'

'We were in his caravan,' said William.

'It's a wonder he let you out. He loves company when he's drinking.'

'We were hoping he might be able to give us something to eat,' William explained.

'Drink is the only thing he takes, and if he doesn't stop soon it'll kill him.'

'I don't suppose you've a slice of bread you could spare?' asked William.

The old man looked around at the table behind him. 'There's a slice or two there. You're welcome to it, but I think it's gone a bit mouldy.'

William left the control box on the table, and James Pius watched as he opened the wrapping paper. There were four slices at the bottom of it, and there were indeed spots of blue-mould on them. However, the two of them were ravenous, and they ate all but the worst affected parts.

'I see you've drawn a line between the two flags,' said the old man. 'A bit like the border, isn't it?'

'My grandfather says that some day unity will come,' said James Pius. 'That it will span the border, just like the rainbow, and draw the two parts of the country together.'

'My father says all this trouble is only driving people

123

farther and farther apart,' said William. He looked at James Pius. 'But of course, there are some who can't see that.'

The old man turned around and left the boat up on the table.

'Do you think there'll ever be peace?' asked William.

The old man thought a long time before answering. Then he told them. 'I don't really know, but I don't think there'll ever be peace until there's understanding.'

'Understanding of what?' asked William.

'Our differences, of course.'

'And do you think there will ever be a united Ireland?' asked James Pius.

'Unity,' the old man replied, 'isn't just a geographical thing. It's the unity of hearts and minds that really counts.'

'And will we ever see that type of unity here in the North?' asked William.

'The type of unity I'm talking about,' said the old man, 'is as hard to find as rainbows of the moon. I know I won't live to see it, but perhaps you might.'

'But there's no such thing as rainbows of the moon,' said James Pius.

'Oh there is,' the old man assured him. 'There is. But like many other things in life, you won't see one unless you look for it . . .'

Chapter Fourteen

The steam had now stopped rising from James Pius's trousers, and they were thinking it was time to go.

'Do you think it's going to be a sunny day?' asked William, mindful of the fact that he was still without his compass and would be relying on the sun to get his bearings.

'Whenever I worked for the big house,' said the old man, 'I relied on the silent forecasters to tell me what the weather was going to be like.'

'James Pius said there were no big houses in this part of the country,' said William. 'He said the land was so bad Cromwell couldn't even give it away.'

The old man laughed. 'He could be right. But when the good Lord gave us bad land, He made up for it by giving us something else.'

'What else?' asked James Pius. 'There's nothing but lakes around here.'

'Precisely, and they're full of fish. The big house I'm talking about had this lake all to itself. George and I worked for them, but that's all gone now.'

'And who were the silent forecasters you were talking about?' asked William.

The old man smiled. 'Oh, you'll think I'm scatty, or batty, or whatever the word is . . .'

'We won't,' William assured him, and James Pius shook his head too.

'Well, I used to have to get up at six o'clock every morning and switch on the boiler, and in the boiler house there was this colony of bats. They hung from the ceiling in clusters, and over the years I found that their pattern on the ceiling was constantly changing.'

'But what's that got to do with the weather?' asked James Pius.

'Everything. You see, if they were evenly separated in ones, about ten inches apart, it meant fine weather. The more even the pattern and the greater the distances between them, the better the weather, and the longer it would last. But if you wanted to know if there was going to be a really long spell of warm weather, you had to watch the young ones.'

'How come?' asked William.

'Well, when the baby bats started swinging from side to side, I always knew that a long spell of warm weather was on the way.'

'And how could you tell if the weather was going to be bad?' asked James Pius.

'When they closed in and formed into pairs, I knew a break in the weather was on the way in ten to twelve hours. And if the mother bat held the baby close and wrapped her wings around it like a shawl, it was a sign that there was a week of bad weather ahead.'

'Sometimes,' he went on, 'they hung from the ceiling in four or five large clusters, like swarming bees, and that was a sure indication of very bad weather ahead, lasting for many days. On rare occasions they all left the ceiling and lined up in straight lines on the rafters. When that happened there was a severe gale coming in eight to ten hours, no matter what the weathermen were saying.'

'But what about today?' asked William. 'Is it going to be sunny?'

The old man glanced at the roof, and looking up they could see a number of bats hanging from the high ceiling. They weren't in clusters, but separated in ones, about ten inches or so apart.

William smiled. 'So it's going to be a good day?' He looked down at the old man and was about to ask him for directions, when he saw that the sleep that had eluded him all night had finally come. Not having the heart to waken him, he moved over to the table and picked up the *Erin go Bragh*. He was also about to take the control box but James Pius got his hand to it first. For a moment they stared at each other without speaking, and then they slipped away, leaving the old man and his silent forecasters to their sleep.

The mist, they found, was as thick as ever. As they followed the path that led away from the house, James Pius thought William had been very smart to go over to the table and take up the boat before he could get to it. William, on the other hand, was pleased that he had the boat for a change. James Pius, he felt, had been getting very possessive about it, and it was time he was shown that he didn't own it, at least not all of it.

To their surprise, the path didn't lead to a road. Instead, it petered out and once more they found themselves in the fields. They stopped, and walked back. However, it wasn't the old man's odd-shaped house that loomed up out of the mist, but a high overgrown hedge.

'We'll never find our way in this mist,' said James Pius.

'Well, we'd better keep going. We're bound to come to a road sooner or later.'

James Pius was getting the feeling that they were going the wrong way again, but he said nothing. He was in no hurry to find a road.

As they made their way cautiously down the hedge, William asked, 'What did you think of the old man?'

'I thought he was very nice.'

'So did I. And imagine telling the weather by the way bats hang from the ceiling.' William reckoned that James Pius had already tried to get away with the boat once, and would probably try again. Privately, therefore, he was hoping that the old man could really tell the weather by looking at the bats, and that it would be a good day. All he needed was the sun to get his bearings, and he would be on his way, hopefully taking the boat with him. 'Do you think he can?'

'Can what?' asked James Pius.

'Tell the weather by looking at the bats?'

James Pius shrugged. It wasn't that he didn't believe the old man; it was more a case of not wanting to believe him. A good day, he knew, was that William wanted. As it was, William had almost succeeded in getting his hands on the boat and the control box at the same time. No, what James Pius reckoned he needed was a cloudy day, away from roads. At least that might give him time to get his hands on the boat again and make off with it before William worked out where he was.

If there was a road in the vicinity, it proved to be as elusive as the will-o-the-wisp. After a while, James Pius stopped. 'This mist is making me wet again. And I don't know about you, but my stomach thinks my throat's cut.'

William nodded. 'Me too. I could eat a horse.'

They kept going, and a short time later came to a river.

'If we follow it, it's bound to bring us to a bridge,' said William. 'Then all we have to do is walk along the road until we meet somebody who can tell us where we are.'

They could see the river quite clearly now, and as they continued along the bank, James Pius observed that he thought the mist was beginning to clear. He was right. A short time later it evaporated and they found themselves walking in the morning sun.

'So the silent forecasters were right!' William smiled. For all his expertise, the officer, he reckoned, wouldn't have been able to tell the weather by looking at bats clinging to a ceiling, and he looked forward to telling him what the old man had said. In the meantime, he must be pushing on. He pointed the hour hand of his watch at the sun, and announced, 'That's due south.'

'I know where we are,' said James Pius.

'How do you mean?'

James Pius hesitated for a moment, then looking around him said, 'We're ... we're back where we started. Look. There's our shelter.'

To his surprise, William saw he was right. They must have travelled in a circle. Running over to the shelter, he left the *Erin go Bragh* in it, and hurried across to where he had put down his fishing line. Leaving the control box beside the boat James Pius joined him, and they watched anxiously as hook after hook was pulled clear of the water.

'Nothing,' said William dejectedly. 'I tell you what you do. Collect some wood for a fire, and I'll check the rabbit snare.'

James Pius nodded, and, spurred on by their hunger, they set about their separate tasks. When they met at the shelter a few minutes later, however, William held the empty snare in his hand, and James Pius knew without being told that there had been nothing in it.

'Looks as if you're going to be eating frog's legs after all,' said James Pius, and he didn't know himself whether he was jesting or not.

William took the frog from his pocket and holding it in the palm of his hand stroked the back of its neck. Then, putting it back, he said, 'There are fish in that river, and if I can't get them one way, I'll get them another.'

'Maybe we should light the fire first,' suggested James Pius, 'so we'll be ready if you do get something.'

William took out his tobacco box and set to work with his flint and steel to get a fire going in the ring of blackened stones that had held their last fire there.

James Pius watched, and as William bent down to blow the smouldering piece of cottonwool, he took the black button compass out of his pocket and tucked it into the tobacco box.

William, he knew, no longer needed it to tell him which direction to take.

Straightening up, William taped on the lid of his tobacco box, and put it back in his pocket. 'I don't know about you, but as soon as I get something to eat I'm going down to the lake to try out the boat. Then I'm off.'

James Pius nodded. 'That's fine with me.' He still didn't know how the ownership of the boat was going to be resolved, but the tone of William's last remark had given him hope. Perhaps William might agree to give up his part of it and go on his way. If that was so, then only one flag would fly from the *Erin go Bragh*, and that would be the Tricolour.

Striker's men, meanwhile, had been cursing the Irish and the Irish weather.

Smith watched the mist condense on the cold steel of his rifle and thought of Brown. He still found it difficult to accept that the body should be left lying out in the woods. 'I don't even know what we're doing in this God-forsaken country,' he complained, 'and I'm sure Brown didn't know.'

'It's no different from any other part of the United Kingdom,' Willoughby told him.

Peacock put on another brew, and was going through his few remaining rations to see what was left. 'Still, I know what he means. It's not really the same as mainland Britain, is it?'

'The people aren't the same either,' continued Smith. 'After all, they are Irish, aren't they, no matter what they say?'

'They're British,' declared Willoughby. 'Why else do you think we're here fighting for them?'

'Tell that to the Catholics in the Falls Road!' said Smith. 'Or Crossmaglen.'

'Tell it to the Paras who went into the Shankill Road in 1973,' said Peacock. 'They found themselves fighting the Protestants.'

'It's funny all right,' Willoughby agreed, 'how some of them are prepared to fight us to stay British and the others are prepared to fight us because they say they're not British.'

'Tea's up,' Peacock announced. He left his rifle down parallel with his legs and stirred powdered milk into his mug.

The others helped themselves, and, leaning back, Smith looked up at the camouflage netting that covered their position. 'Mannering says Brown didn't know what hit him.'

Before they knew it, Striker had slipped in beside them. 'You won't either if you don't stay alert. And don't leave that rifle out of your hand, any of you.'

'But we can't see a thing, Sarge,' said Willoughby. 'That's a real peasouper out there.'

'Talking about soup, Sarge,' said Peacock, 'our rations are running a bit low.'

Striker looked at him and nodded. 'Just keep your eyes skinned. I'll get you something that'll keep you going until we get back to base.' He turned to Willoughby who was working at his radio set. 'Any messages?'

'Nothing.'

Striker was gone as silently as he had come, and Peacock said, 'I wonder where he disappears to?'

'Probably across the river trying to locate the Hawk,' Willoughby told him. 'Isn't that what the SAS are trained to do, operate behind enemy lines?'

Smith shivered. 'Rather him than me.'

When Striker returned, he had a steaming mess tin in his hand. 'It's not tea and toast, but it'll warm you up, and it's full of protein.'

They shared it out, and when Striker had gone, Peacock said, 'It's not like breakfast in bed either.'

'First time I had stew for my breakfast,' grumbled Smith. 'I wonder what's in it?'

'It's very tasty,' said Willoughby, 'and it's warm. Now eat up before it goes cold.'

'Oxtail soup for breakfast,' said Peacock. 'Wait until my missus hears about this.'

Smith hadn't taken any of it yet. 'What are all these short red stringy pieces?'

'Meat of some sort, I imagine,' said Willoughby. 'Why, what do you think it is?'

'I was just thinking about some of the things Mannering said. You know, about what these SAS chaps eat when they run out of food.'

'You mean like rats?' asked Peacock.

'And worms.' Smith was holding up one of the short stringy pieces. 'They're high in protein, aren't they?'

Peacock put down his mess tin, and stirred the remains of his stew with his spoon.

'It's full of all those little red stringy things, isn't it,' said Smith.

Willoughby, who had just put a spoonful in his mouth, spat it out and wiped his mouth on the back of his hand. 'Smith, you'd put anyone off his food. You're disgusting, that's what you are.'

'Striker wouldn't do that to us, would he?' Peacock looked at the other two, and seeing the look on their faces put his finger down his throat and made himself throw up.

'What's wrong with you then?' Peacock looked up to see Striker looking at him. 'Got a tummy bug?'

'Something like that, Sarge.'

'Well then, take a tablet ... and why aren't you two eating?'

'What's in it, Sarge?' asked Smith.

'Oxtail soup and stewed steak. Why? Something wrong with it?'

'No,' said Willougby, 'just a bit early in the morning for it, that's all.' He turned around to cover his embarrassment and trained his field-glasses on the river. 'Mist's clearing.'

Striker took the glasses and put them to his eyes. 'That's

strange, the boys are back.'

'I didn't know they were away,' said Willoughby.

'I went down there under cover of the mist,' Striker told him. 'Thought I might be able to get my hands on the boat. But they had gone.' He gave the glasses back to Willoughby. 'Anyway, the important thing is, they're back. And if I'm not mistaken, it won't be long before the Hawk is back too.'

Smith reached behind and quietly emptied out the contents of his mess tin. 'Do you think we should dig in then, Sarge?'

Striker shook his head. 'No. He won't make the same mistake twice.'

'What do you plan to do?' asked Willoughby.

'Do you see the ruins of that old cottage?' When Willoughyby peered through the field –glasses, Striker continued, 'There are two of them in there.'

Peacock and Smith came forward now to have a look, and Peacock said, 'Why don't we go over and lob a few grenades in on top of them?'

'Because we don't know where the Hawk is,' Striker told him, 'and because it would make the boys take off again. Sooner or later their luck is going to run out, and when it does that bomb's going to go off.'

'So what do you want us to do?' asked Willoughby.

Striker picked up his own radio and strapped it on to his shoulders. 'I want you and Smith to keep an eye on those ruins. If you see the Hawk or anyone else joining them, let me know.'

Willoughby looked through the glasses at the ruins again. 'Then what, Sarge?'

'When I give the word, open fire and keep them pinned down. That should give me enough time to get the boat and get out.'

'I can't wait,' said Smith, propping his rifle up on its bi-pod.

133

'Peacock,' Striker continued, 'you join Mannering in the other OP and tell him what I've said. And stay alert, all of you. I don't know what the Hawk is up to, but he wants that boat just as badly as we do, so you can bet your sweet life he's up to something.'

Chapter Fifteen

The sun was shining on the river, and the birds were singing in the trees, almost as if they too were celebrating the lifting of the mist and the arrival of a glorious day. Here and there, small circles rippled outwards on the water, but neither William nor James Pius needed these tell-tale signs to tell them that trout were feeding. They could see them clearly in the sunlight, their brown bodies waving sinuously as they faced into the current or circled a stone, now and then popping up to pluck an insect from the surface.

'That's why they didn't go for the worms,' said James Pius. 'Too many flies.'

William, who had just baited his hooks with several minnows which he had trapped in the plastic bottle, nodded. 'They probably won't take the minnows either, but we'll see what happens.'

'We'll starve to death if we have to wait much longer.' James Pius was still gazing into the river. 'I tell you what. I know another way we might catch one. Lend me your snare and I'll show you.'

Suddenly a voice behind them demanded. 'James Pius! What are you doing here?'

Startled, they turned around to find themselves face to face with a black-haired girl in a navy cardigan, white blouse and jeans.

'Martina!' exclaimed James Pius.

'I asked you what you were doing here?' she continued.

'You're supposed to be at grandfather's.'

'Ah, this is William.'

James Pius was suddenly aware that she was looking at William's army outfit and said hastily, 'Don't worry, he's not a Brit, although he's not far off it.' He pointed towards the shelter. 'We found a boat . . . and, ah, we got lost in the mist.'

'Lost?' she asked, ignoring William.

'Aye, we got lost,' repeated James Pius, and stepping closer he gave her a nudge on the arm with his elbow.

Martina looked at William now, and when he held out his hand again she shook it, saying, 'Sorry. I'm his sister.'

William smiled. 'No need to be sorry. It could happen to anybody.'

A faint smile crossed her face, and James Pius grunted, 'Huh! Very funny. He's a Prod you know. That's his Union Jack on the boat.'

Martina lowered her eyes, and taking her hand back walked with them over to the shelter.

Lifting up the *Erin go Bragh*, James Pius nodded towards the Tricolour. 'That's my half.'

Martina looked at the Union Jack, and the words 'Ulster Says No' scribbled on the bow. 'And I suppose that's your half?'

William nodded, and waited for a caustic remark.

Whatever her feelings, however, Martina kept them to herself. Instead, she watched James Pius place the boat back in the shelter. Then she turned to William again and asked, 'What are you two doing here?'

William reckoned she was about the same age as he was, maybe slightly younger, but not much. Her black hair, which was held back by a white band, glinted in the sun, and her skin was sallow, but clear, not like her brother's. In fact, he thought she was quite attractive. 'We're going to try out the boat, then we'll be on our way.'

'We found it on . . . on one of the lakes,' said James Pius.

136

'The Brits and the Provos were having a go at each other and I think the man who owned it must have got hit.'

'We'll see if we can get it going as soon as we can get something to eat,' said William. 'We've had very little to eat since we lost our bearings.' He looked at James Pius. 'And then my compass disappeared.'

Martina looked at her brother, wondering what was going on, but he just shrugged and said, 'I haven't got it.'

William got out his sheath knife and was turning to go down the river bank, when James Pius said, 'Are you going to lend me that snare or not?'

William opened his box and gave it to him.

'I'll need that string as well.'

Placing the box on the ground, William knelt down to untangle the string, 'What are you going to do with it.'

'Something my grandfather told me he did once. I want to see if it works. What are you going to do?'

'I'm going down as far as the sallies.'

'What are you two trying to do?' asked Martina.

'The trout won't take our bait,' William explained. 'So we're going to try something else.' He looked at James Pius. 'I won't be far away. If you see a tug on the minnows, give me a wave. I'll be able to see you from where I am.'

James Pius nodded. 'And I'll just be over there — at the edge of the trees.'

Martina said nothing, but she knew this was their way of saying they'd be keeping an eye on each other. She reckoned there had been quite a lot of aggro between the two of them, and she intended to find out just what had been going on. For the moment, however, she decided to sit down and watch the trout.

Just inside the trees, James Pius searched around until he found a bundle of sticks which someone had cut, perhaps for thatching, and then forgotten about. They were straight and weathered, but not rotten, and he selected a fairly long one. His grandfather had told him that once, when he was on the run, he had snared a trout and now James Pius was going to try and do the same. The idea was to tie the string to the end of the snare, and then bring it up along the stick like the line on a fishing rod. He really could have done with William's knife, but wouldn't please him by asking for it.

William, meanwhile, had gone down the river a short distance to a spot not far from the lake, where the reeds gave way to various types of bushes, including one known locally as black sally. There he was preparing to try out something equally as bizarre; he was going to try and spear a fish.

However, while the officer had shown him how to make the spears, he hadn't told him what wood to use. As a result he now had to find wood that was easy enough to split, but strong enough not to split too far.

At a glance, it appeared to him that the branches of the sally weren't as straight or as firm as the ones the officer had brought to his house. Nor did they look as brown. Cutting off a branch which he thought might serve his purpose, he split the end and then pushed the handle of the knife into the split. Just as he thought, too soft.

Farther along he cut a branch from a different kind of sally, and was just stripping off the leaves when he became aware of Martina standing beside him.

Picking up one of the twigs, she said, 'That's a funny place for seeds to grow.'

'Where?'

'Under the leaves, look.'

'They're not seeds,' said William, 'they're galls. I'd say some sort of fly lays its eggs under the leaves, and those things grow up around them.'

Martina sat down beside him. 'You seem to know an awful lot about nature.'

'My Uncle Robert taught me a lot of things. He was a farmer.'

Martina looked at him. 'Was?'

William nodded. 'The IRA killed him.'

'Was he in the security forces?'

William didn't answer.

'Was it a mistake?'

'It was no mistake.'

'My brother Seamus was killed by the security forces,' said Martina, 'and they said that was a mistake. We didn't believe them.'

Neither felt it appropriate to elaborate further on the killings.

William split the sally somewhat more viciously than he had intended, dividing it almost to the end. 'It's all a mistake. Why can't people live and let live?'

'What are you doing?'

'I'm looking for something I can use to spear fish.'

Martina grimaced and gave a slight shiver.

'But this wood's too soft.' William got up and moved over into the woods. There he cut a branch of birch and as he sat down on a fallen tree, Martina joined him.

Thinking of what he had written on the boat, she asked, 'What have Protestants got against being Irish?'

William stripped the branch of its leaves. 'We are Irish, but we're British as well. I told your brother that.'

'But what have you got against a united Ireland? I mean, what have you got against the Free State?'

'If we went into a united Ireland, we'd be run by the Catholic Church, just the way they are down there.'

'But they're not run by the Catholic Church,' said Martina. 'Freedom of religion is guaranteed in the Constitution, no matter what you are.'

William split the end of the branch. 'Then how come they wouldn't allow divorce when the Protestants wanted it?'

'A lot of Catholics wanted it too, but when they held a referendum the majority of people said no.' Martina picked up a twig and started pulling off the leaves. 'Anyway, it would be different in a united Ireland. You'd have all these things if you wanted them.'

'But we have them now, and so have you.' William got up, walked over to a rowanberry tree and examined it for a straight branch.

Martina followed and plucked a bunch of rowanberries. 'I still can't understand it.'

'Understand what?'

'Why anyone would want to be British instead of Irish.'

'Our whole tradition is British,' William told her. 'My father's family all fought for Britain in the last war. One of his uncles was killed in it. It was war dead like him that the people were commemorating at Enniskillen when the IRA blew them up.'

Martina was about to say that was a mistake too, but thought it better to change the subject. 'You and James Pius didn't get on very well, did you?' He didn't answer, and she continued, 'He can be a terrible brat sometimes.' She paused, before adding, 'But then he has good reason to be.'

Pulling down a branch, William nicked it above and below so that it would break off cleanly. 'He isn't really lost, is he?'

She shook her head. 'I'd say he got lost in the mist all right, but he knows roughly where he is.'

'I thought so, otherwise you wouldn't have been able to find him.'

'That was just luck. I'm going to my grandfather's too, but I had to take a roundabout route. There's been a lot of shooting along the way we normally go, and we think the Brits may have been blowing up some of the bridges.'

William nodded. 'That would explain why he didn't seem to know any of the people we met.'

'I wouldn't know them either,' said Martina. 'But are you not afraid he'll run off with the boat, now that we're out of sight?'

'It's not much good without the control box, and I have that.' He took the black box out of his pocket and showed it to her.

Martina looked at the box, then at him, saying, 'You know, you're as bad as he is, maybe worse.'

'Well, I've as much right to it as he has.'

'It would serve you right if you both lost it. I've a good mind to take it myself, just to spite the two of you!'

William grunted and smiled, then discarding the rowan-berry branch, he went over to a clump of hazels, cut out a long straight branch and sat down on the grass.

Martina adjusted her hairband and looked down at him. He was the first Protestant boy she had met, and she reckoned he could be just as big a brat as her brother. Nevertheless, she was beginning to like him. 'There's no reason why we shouldn't be friends, is there?'

William stopped cutting, and looked up at her. 'But you're a ...'

'A Catholic? And what if I am? I haven't got two heads, have I?' She paused. 'Anyway, I only asked you if we could be friends. I'm not asking you to marry me!'

William continued with his cutting, and lowered his head as he felt his face getting red. 'Sorry.'

'Anyway, what's wrong with marrying a Catholic if it comes to that?'

'Nothing. It's just that Catholics want their children brought up Catholics.'

'And what's wrong with that?'

William split the end of the hazel branch and finding that it held well, got up and selected several more straight branches. 'If the children of all mixed marriages are brought up Catholics, that means less and less Protestants.'

'If they're brought up Protestants,' countered Martina, 'that means less Catholics.'

'But there are a lot less of us, especially in the South.'

'Maybe so,' said Martina, 'but there are less of us up here in the North.'

William split the ends of the branches and inserted short plugs into the splits, thus widening them out into two-pronged and four-pronged spears. 'Anyway, where I come from, we think the children of mixed marriages should be brought up in the same religion as the father. That way it would be fair, and no religion would suffer.'

'And what about the mother? Does she have no say in it?'

William had no intention of getting any deeper into the argument, so he started cutting notches near the end of the spear tips to provide them with a barb that would hold the trout.

Seeing that he wasn't going to be drawn on the matter further, Martina said, 'You know, this is the first time I've ever talked to a Protestant.'

'Why, did you think we had two heads?'

Martina smiled. 'I suppose I asked for that.'

'Sorry. You're the first Catholic girl I've ever talked to. You'd think we lived on different planets, wouldn't you?'

Martina nodded.

William opened his tobacco box, and as he rooted through his bits and pieces, he was aware that her nose was twitching. However, she didn't ask what the sweet smell was. Maybe, he thought, it was because she was wearing perfume and didn't notice. It was nice perfume.

'Seems an awful lot of trouble just to catch a fish.'

'Not if you're as hungry as we are.' William got up and there was a glint in his eye. 'All right, if we're going to be friends, hold that for me.'

Martina held out her hand and he placed the frog on her palm. Being a country girl, it wasn't the first time she had held a frog in her hand. However, she got such a fright that she screamed. At the same time she pulled her hand back so quickly that the frog went flying through the air.

James Pius had just completed his makeshift rod when he heard the scream. Thinking something was wrong he rushed down, only to find Martina walloping William on the back of the shoulders with one of his spears.

'That was a dirty, rotten trick,' she was shouting at him. She hit him a few more times. 'A dirty, rotten trick.'

William turned, and he was laughing so much the tears were running down his cheeks.

'What did you do to her?' James Pius demanded.

'He did nothing to me,' scowled Martina. 'He just gave me a fright with that frog.'

William searched around until he located the frog and put it back in his pocket.

'Don't tell me you're still going to eat it?' said James Pius.

'Eat the frog?' shouted Martina, and for a moment James Pius thought she was going to give him a wallop too. 'You're disgusting, James Pius. You're every bit as bad as he is.'

Smiling to himself at the good of it all, William walked back up to the shelter, and anxious to escape his sister's wrath James Pius hurried after him.

The sun was higher in the sky now, and it was getting warm. The trout, they could see, were still moving around the bed of the river, as big and as tempting as ever. Within a few minutes, James Pius was sitting, still as a statue, on a rock a short distance out from the bank, waiting for a trout to swim into his snare, while William lay on the bank, his spear poised, ready to strike. The fish had scattered as they moved into position, but with a bit of luck, they'd be back.

Martina had moved the flat stone into the centre of the fire, just in case they did catch something, and when there was no move from either of them she crawled over beside William. 'Any luck?'

William shook his head. 'Still mad?'

Martina smiled and shook her head. The joke with the frog was just the sort of thing James Pius would do, and she thought how much alike the two boys were when it came to things like that, despite their very different backgrounds.

'They're just starting to come back,' William whispered. 'Be careful you don't cast your shadow on the water, or you'll frighten them away.'

'I'm sure you're not allowed to catch fish like that.'

'Probably not,' whispered William. 'But we're starving, so the law will just have to make allowances.'

'Shussh,' said James Pius. He pulled on the string and yanked out the snare. To their surprise, the others saw a good-sized trout hanging by its tail. As it jerked around trying to get free, James Pius seized it and triumphantly brought it back to the bank.

Pleased as he was at the prospect of eating, William didn't want to be outdone, so he gave James Pius his knife, saying, 'Here. You get it ready. I'll see if I can get another one.'

Soon, however, William found that spearing a fish wasn't as easy as the army officer had suggested. Each time he plunged in his spear he missed, even though he was certain he was on target. It was only after he realised that the water was showing the fish in a slightly different position from where they actually were, that he succeeded in getting one. Then he discovered it wasn't as big as it appeared to have been either. Nevertheless, honour was satisfied.

Soon their appetites were satisfied too, and they were ready to go down to the lake to try out the *Erin go Bragh*.

Chapter Sixteen

The mist had long since lifted, and fingers of sunlight were probing the briars of the old cottage when Cathal Óg and the Professor heard the sound of a tractor. Crawling over to what had been the back wall of the cottage, they saw a farmer driving down the field to the edge of the sallies. There he lifted several bundles of reeds which had been cut and tied like stooks of corn, and threw them into a high-sided trailer.

'I don't think it's Mickey Joe,' said Cathal Óg.

The Professor nodded and pushed his glasses back up on his nose. 'I thought it might have been him bringing the mortars. Better keep out of sight.'

They sat down again, their backs to the gable wall, their Kalashnikovs cradled in their laps. A few minutes later, they heard the farmer start up the tractor again, move on and stop.

'Must be collecting more reeds,' whispered Cathal Óg.

The tractor started up once more, and they held their breath as it drew closer, then came to a stop outside. Cathal Óg pulled back the cocking hand of his rifle, and knowing the noise it would make if he released it, quietly but firmly pushed it forward into position. The Professor did likewise, and moving as quickly as the briars would allow them they flattened themselves into the corners of the ruin and peered out.

The trailer, they could see, had come to a stop immediately opposite and not knowing what to expect, they were just about to get into a firing position when they heard Seamus saying, 'It's a friend of Mickey Joe's.' At the same time they saw him hopping off the back of the trailer. Pausing momentarily to reach back for a rucksack, he scrambled in over the rubble and sat back against the gable wall.

'How's the arm?' asked the Professor.

'Sore enough, but I got it cleaned and dressed.'

'But can you use it?' asked Cathal Óg.

Knowing he meant could he shoot with it, Seamus opened the rucksack, and taking out a walkie-talkie radio said, 'You can do the shooting. I'll operate this.'

'What's Sean got in mind?' asked the Professor.

Seamus took a roll of cottonwool, a bandage and a small bottle from the rucksack and handed it to him. 'Here's some antiseptic. Better put a clean dressing on yourself.'

Cathal Óg had the field-glasses to his eyes, and was looking out towards the river.

'Are the boys still there?' asked Seamus.

'They are, and there's a girl there now too.'

Seamus went over to have a look. 'Mmmm. Must be trying to catch themselves some breakfast.' He gave the field-glasses back to Cathal Óg and reaching into the rucksack again said, 'Here, I brought you some food.'

'What's he got in mind?' asked the Professor again.

'The mortars are in the trailer,' said Seamus. 'As soon as you're ready, we'll get into it too and move into position.'

Seamus began talking into the walkie-talkie, and a few moments later they heard the whispered voice of Sean the Hawk coming back to them, asking for an up-date on the situation.

'There's a girl with them now,' said Seamus.

'I know. It's Ned's daughter.'

Seamus and Cathal Óg looked at the Professor. They said nothing, but they knew that the presence of the girl now placed him in real danger. For, whatever about the boy, the death of the girl would almost certainly mean the Hawk

146

would carry out his threat.

The Hawk was still speaking on the radio. 'Striker has changed his position again. You do the same, and don't delay. Get set up, and I'll see if I can pin-point his new position.'

'Then what?' asked Seamus.

'My guess is the boys will move down to the lake to try out the boat. If they get it out far enough without blowing themselves up, I'll have a go at it. You give me covering fire with the mortar when I say the word.'

The Professor took the walkie-talkie. 'You want to be very careful. If it's coming towards you, remember, it's directional.'

'Don't worry, I won't forget.'

The others looked at the Professor again. They knew by the tone of the Hawk's voice that he was also saying he wouldn't forget who to blame if anything went wrong.

The Professor got up. 'Come on so. We'll get the mortar set up inside the trailer. Its high sides will hide us and the floor will give us a firm base for firing. It'll also give us the mobility we need if we have to change position in a hurry.'

James Pius walked down the river bank towards the lake. The *Erin go Bragh* was under his arm, and there was a spring in his step. Possession, he was saying to himself, was nine tenths of the law. He didn't quite know yet how he was going to assert that possession, but he would do it somehow. One way or another, the boat would be his ... not just part of it, but all of it. The Union Jack would be removed, the Tricolour would stay, and the line that William had drawn across it would be erased.

Martina and William walked side by side a short distance behind him, and there was a spring in their step too, but for a different reason. In spite of their differences, they were enjoying each other's company.

As Martina had said, William was the first Protestant boy

she had ever met. She couldn't understand some of the arguments he had made, especially about marriage and divorce, but she liked him. He was tall and handsome, and he had a sense of humour. She had been led to believe that Protestants, or at least some of them, led such a strict life they didn't even watch television and for that reason she had the impression that they didn't get any fun out of life. William's prank with the frog had, therefore, surprised her, and while it had annoyed her at the time she had come to see the funny side of it.

As they walked along, the sun shone warmly on them. Blue tits flitted furtively about in the depths of the sallies, and a gentle breeze rippled through the tall green reeds. Here and there between the clumps of reeds they could see the large heart-shaped leaves of water lilies floating just beneath the surface, while a short distance across, near the opposite shore, grew the lilies themselves, not yellow, but pristine white in the morning sun.

It was a morning, thought William, that made the events of the previous day seem distant, their nightmare in the mist unreal, the bickering with James Pius almost unimportant. Even when he wasn't looking at Martina, he was conscious of her walking along beside him. He was continually aware of her presence, and it pleased him that she was there. He smiled as he thought of the fright he had given her with the frog, and while she didn't agree with some of the things he had said, at least she didn't seem to despise him for having views that were different to hers. Not like James Pius. She was also very pretty, he thought. What a pity they couldn't continue to be friends. But there was no way they could, not with their different backgrounds, their different religions. Too many things had happened. Death had laid its hand on both families and while some day time might allow them to forgive, it would not allow them to forget.

For the moment, however, the lake which had held so

much danger for James Pius and himself in the early morning, sparkled in the sunlight like an oasis of peace in a country torn by bitterness and strife. Little did they know that as James Pius prepared to place the *Erin go Bragh* in the water, the forces of violence were gathering once again, and the danger was greater than ever before.

'How do you make it go?' asked Martina.

'This switch in here starts it,' James Pius told her. He demonstrated by starting up the propeller, and then switched it off again. 'All we have to do is to find out how to steer it.'

William pushed the switch on the control box to 'on' and the needle under the glass dial moved up to green. 'It must have something to do with the switches.'

Martina watched her brother place the boat in the water, and flick another switch he had found under the cabin roof. Nothing happened, and as he felt around to see if there were any more switches, William said, 'Hold on a minute ... maybe the aerial's not high enough.'

From the sallies on the far side of the lake, Sean the Hawk watched them anxiously.

'What are they doing now?' the Professor asked him on the walkie-talkie.

'They've extended the aerial on the control box.'

'Anything else?'

'They're working at the switches. What do you think?'

'It depends on the controls. What position they have them in.'

The Professor said no more, and Sean the Hawk knew from his silence that inside the boat the small plastic starfish he had told them about must now be flicking dangerously close to the micro-switch that would detonate the bomb.

Unknown to the Hawk, Striker was also watching what was going on from the woods opposite.

'Any move from the cottage?' he was asking Willoughby

149

on the radio.

'Negative,' came the reply. 'The only thing we saw was a farmer with a tractor and trailer.'

'What was he doing?'

'Gathering rushes, as far as we could see.'

'Did he go near the cottage?'

Willoughby paused. 'I think he stopped on the far side of it. Why, Sarge?'

Striker sighed. 'Where is he now?'

'Can't see him. Probably down at the edge of the sallies collecting more rushes. Why, is it important?'

'Could be. Keep your eyes skinned.'

As Striker and the Hawk now trained their field-glasses on the three young people and the boat from opposite directions, they got a fleeting glimpse of each other's face in the undergrowth. Instinctively, they raised their rifles and ducked. However, there was nothing they could do. Even if they disregarded the three young people working with the boat on the lake shore, and opened fire on each other, there was the danger that a stray bullet would detonate the bomb and that suited neither of them. Nor were they in a position to call in the covering fire they had planned, as it was obvious that both units were on the move. It was a classic case of what military people called a Mexican stand-off, a situation in which neither side could open fire. Realising this, they immediately changed their positions.

Unaware of what was going on either in front of them or behind them, James Pius and William were still trying to find the right combination of switches and levers to get the *Erin go Bragh* going.

'Try that lever there,' suggested Martina.

'I've already tried it,' said William.

'Well, try it again.'

William moved the joystick on the right back and forth, and to their delight they found it now moved the rudder from

150

side to side. The little lever behind it, they found, also moved the rudder slightly.

James Pius lifted the boat out of the water, saying, 'See if you can get the rudder to stay in the centre. Otherwise it'll go round in circles.'

William worked at the joystick and the smaller lever until James Pius told him, 'That's it, that's it. Leave it there.'

Martina was almost dancing with excitement. 'Start it up. Start it up.'

James Pius flicked the switch beside the small imitation steering-wheel, and as the tiny propeller whirred into life again he pushed the boat into the water.

It immediately moved off, and William cried, 'Look, I can make it go whatever way I want!' He moved the joystick to the right, and the boat turned around in a tight circle in front of them.

In the sallies opposite, Sean the Hawk watched and prayed that the bomb wouldn't go off, at least not until it was farther out into the lake.

'Here, let me try it,' said James Pius, taking the control box and pointing the aerial at the boat. 'I wonder how far it'll go?' He put the joystick in the centre position and they watched as it headed out into the lake.

On the far side, Sean the Hawk trained his Kalashnikov on the boat and waited. He didn't want to open fire unless he had to. Apart from the danger of hitting Ned's youngsters, he would also be betraying his new position now, and if there was a clear line of fire the sallies would offer him no protection. However, he needn't have worried.

'Here, let me try it,' said Martina.

'No, it's not your boat, it's mine,' replied James Pius.

'It's as much my boat as it is yours,' William reminded him. 'I say we let her have a go at it.'

Reluctantly, James Pius handed his sister the control box. Flicking the joystick on the right, Martina watched excitedly as she turned the boat around in a circle again.

'Keep it going,' urged James Pius. 'I want to see how far it'll go out.'

Martina ignored him. 'I wonder what these controls on the left are for?' She moved the small lever into the centre, and looked at the boat. Nothing happened.

'Move the big one,' suggested James Pius.

Still watching the boat, Martina flicked the second joystick to the right. Immediately a deafening explosion tore up the centre of the lake, sending a huge tower of white water into the sky.

At the same time, a hail of shrapnel went whistling across the sallies, as the boat-bomb unleashed its deadly cargo. Instinctively they ducked. Then, looking up, they saw a brilliant rainbow in the spray as the sun reflected on a million drops of falling water.

For what seemed an age, but was really only an instant, they clung together, united in awe at the terrible beauty of what they saw, and in the realisation that what had been fought for so jealously might well have been the means of their own destruction. A moment later, the rainbow was gone, and so was the *Erin go Bragh*. Not even its name remained on the heaving surface of the water.

Martina, her face white with shock and anger, pushed her brother away and screamed at him, 'That was a bomb you were carrying! You might have got us all killed.'

James Pius was shaking like a leaf. 'How was I to know,' he shouted back at her. 'We just found it on the lake.'

William tried to stop himself trembling. 'That's right.' Realising that he too was shouting, he lowered his voice and assured her, 'He's right. We had no idea it was a bomb.'

'We thought it was an ordinary boat,' shivered James Pius.

Martina took a deep breath as she tried to compose herself. 'Well you might have got us all killed. Wait until you get home, you'll get what for.'

'You better not say anything about it, or we'll both get into trouble,' warned James Pius. 'Anyway, I'm going to grandfather's place.' He looked up and around. 'We'd better go before the Brits come in to find out what's going on.'

'Or the IRA,' said William. 'It must have been their bomb.'

James Pius headed off. 'Come on, Martina.'

Martina ignored him. Instead she turned to William and he could see she had almost succeeded in calming herself. 'I suppose you're off now too?' she said.

He nodded, and taking the frog from his pocket, set it in the long grass at the edge of the water. For a moment it sat still. Then, realising it was free, it hopped across the grass and disappeared.

The two of them looked at each other and smiled.

'Maybe we'll meet again some time,' she said.

'I'd like that.'

Even as they spoke, however, they realised that they were looking at each other across a great divide, a divide not of their own making, but one created by centuries of political and religious dissension.

'Come on,' shouted James Pius. 'Are you coming or not?'

'All right, I'm coming.' Martina joined him, and as she paused to wave good-bye to William she felt she really would like to meet him again. However, she knew in her heart and soul that it was most unlikely. She also knew it was even more unlikely that James Pius and he would ever meet again. At the moment, she could see, they had nothing more to say to each other, not even good-bye. But then, as they grew older and circumstances changed, who could tell what might happen? Her only hope was that if the two of them ever did see each other again, it would be as friends, and not across the barrel of a gun.

The sound of helicopters came to their ears now, and they hurried on their separate ways.

Author's Note

In 1984, a small quantity of white powder was found among bomb-making materials in a house in County Dublin. Forensic examination showed that it was the military high-explosive RDX. The gardai immediately notified the RUC and Scotland Yard and a search was begun for what media reports at the time called the IRA 'scientist' who had found out how to make it.

For some reason, the IRA does not appear to have gone ahead with production of the explosive. Perhaps the importation of large quantities of Semtex from Libya during the following two years — prior to the seizure of the *Eksund* — rendered the production of RDX unnecessary.

It was also during those years that the IRA smuggled in large quantities of Kalashnikov assault rifles, such as those that feature in this story, and, as I write, the nationwide search for them continues.

While *Rainbows of the Moon* is a work of fiction, it required a certain amount of research, and all those I approached for information and advice were most helpful. In thanking them I am not, of course, suggesting for one moment that they share any of the views expressed in the story.

Among the military people who were of assistance to me were Major David Winn of the British Army Information Service in Lisburn, County Antrim, Commandant Dave Ashe of the Defence Forces Press Office in Dublin, and two former members of that office, Commandant Peter Burns and

Commandant Declan Carbery.

There are some military personnel and others who, because of the specialist nature of their work, I cannot acknowledge by name. For their help I am especially grateful and I trust they will accept this form of acknowledgment as a sincere 'thank you' for all they did to acquaint me with certain technical and scientific matters.

For background information on the Orange Order, the Royal Arch Purple and the Royal Black Institution, I would like to acknowledge *The Chosen Few* by Anthony D. Buckley, from *Folk Life*, and *Brotherhoods in Ireland* by the same writer and Kenneth Anderson, published by the Ulster Folk and Transport Museum, Cultra, County Down.

The large tapestries depicting King William, sword in hand and on a chestnut charger at the Battle of the Boyne, and King James surveying the beleagured City of Londonderry are, of course, a feature of the House of Lords which is preserved in the old parliament building in College Green, Dublin, by the Bank of Ireland. It was many years since I had seen them, and I am grateful to Harry O'Riordan and his colleague, Brendan Comer, for affording me the opportunity of having another look at them. The point has been made by other writers that King William is always depicted on a white horse on Orange banners because a white horse was the emblem of the Protestant House of Hanover.

The story of the Mace of the House of Commons, which is still preserved in the House of Lords, and of the refusal of the last Speaker to hand it over after the Act of Union, is told in *Sixty Golden Moments*, a walking tour guide of Dublin from the Bank of Ireland, College Green, written by Eamonn Mac Thomais.

The suggestion made by William in *Rainbows of the Moon* that the Pope said prayers for the success of King William at the Battle of the Boyne may be traced to the fact that following the battle, news of the victory was quickly forwarded to King William's allies in the Grand Alliance, and the Pope is said to have given his consent to *Te Deums* (a Latin hymn of praise) being sung in the Catholic cathedrals of Austria and Spain. The Alliance was formed by both Protestant and Catholic rulers determined to prevent the political and military ambitions of France's Louis XIV to dominate Europe, and as King James was backed by the French there was great rejoicing throughout the Alliance at his defeat.

On this point, Peter Berresford Ellis writes in his book *The Boyne Water* (Blackstaff Press 1989) — 'A rumour went around that a *Te Deum* was sung in St. Peter's in Rome and had Pope Innocent XI, the bitter enemy of Louis XIV, who had helped finance William's army, still been alive, it in all probability would have been. But the new Pope Alexander VIII was less hostile to France than Innocent had been and John Drummond, first earl of Melfort, reported that the new Pope was scandalised by the *Te Deums* sung in Catholic cathedrals to celebrate the victory.'

In his account of the battle, the same writer says the first regiment into the attack, i.e. the main attack at Oldbridge, were the three battalions of William's *corps d'elite*, the Dutch Blue Guards. 'The march that the fifes and drums of the Dutch Blue Guards chose to play was the ever popular *Lillebulero*. The jaunty strains of the music must have rankled in the ears of the Irish Jacobites as it carried across the river.'

Lillibulero was a satirical ballad composed by Whig politician Thomas Wharton when King James nominated General Richard Talbot, Earl of Tyrconnell, to be Lord Lieutenant in Ireland, the first Catholic viceroy for over a hundred years. In a reference to the two of them, Wharton's ballad said in part:

> *Dere was an old prophecy found in a bog*
> *Lillibuléro bullen a la,*

156

> *Dat our land would be ruled by an ass and a dog,*
> *Lillibuléro bullen a la . . .*

Within weeks of being set to music, it was being sung all over Ireland, England and Scotland, and Wharton is quoted as saying it whistled James out of three Kingdoms.

According to the introduction to the ballad in *Rich and Rare* by Sean McMahon (Ward River Press, 1984), the refrain is a mocking parody of the Catholic watchcry during the rising of 1641 and probably means *An lile bá léir é, ba linne an lá*, meaning, *The lily prevailed; the day was ours.*

Both *Lillibulero* and *Bullen a la* also appear to have been used as passwords by Loyalists during their struggles.

For some basic hints on survival, my thanks to Captain Brendan Rohan, Corporal Tommy Quinn and Private Jim Quinn, Stephens Barracks, Kilkenny.

Captain Rohan has also helped young people to prepare for survival courses in connection with the President's Award, and I would like to thank some of those who talked to me about their experiences. They included Anne O'Connor of Ardscoil la Salle, Raheny, Dublin, and several boys from Ardscoil Rís, Griffith Avenue, Dublin — David Roberts, who was good enough to share with me the secrets of his "Golden Virginia" survival box, Sean Duffy, Damien Vizzard, Kieran Fleming, Damien Creagh and Tony Brady. My thanks also to two other students at Ardscoil Rís, Mark Byrne and Eoin Ennis, who told me about their adventures while orienteering in the West. I am grateful to the boys' PE teacher, Liam Moggan, for arranging a meeting with them, and giving me additional information about their participation in the scheme.

Several members of the Gárda Siochana also helped me in certain ways, including Superintendent Denis Mullins of the Gárda Press Office and Detective-Inspector Michael Nyland of the Gárda Ballistics Section, now retired.

When, with members of my family, I visited the border areas of Cavan and Leitrim to do some research, Denis Breen of Ballinamore was good enough to take us to various lakes, thus giving me a glimpse of local wildlife, and introducing me to some of the skills of coarse fishing. My thanks to him and his family for their hospitality; also to Francis McGolderick of the Anglers' Rest in Ballyconnell who told me about the fishing in his area.

For the information on the bats, I must thank the family of the late John Collins, of Cong, County Mayo, a writer of letters to the papers, poetry and songs. Part of his work was to switch on a boiler every morning at Ashford Castle, and in an article entitled *The Silent Forecasters*, he recalled how he had studied a colony of bats which slept on the ceiling of the small boiler house.

'The first thing I noticed when entering this room when the bats were there,' he wrote, 'was a strong and strange smell which I have named the "herd scent". The second thing which drew my attention was the constantly changing pattern on the ceiling.

'In Joyce country, around Lough Nafooey, if a farmer wants to know if it will be a suitable day for bringing home his turf or bringing in his hay, he looks at the sheep grazing on the mountainside at about 9 o'clock in the morning and again one hour later, and if they have gone higher up and spread out it will be a fine day, but if they have descended to a lower level and closed in it will surely rain that day.'

Having studied the bats at close quarters, Mr. Collins obviously thought very highly of them and expressed the hope that all of us would learn to love and not fear what he called 'the silent forecasters'.

Aidan Brady, Director of the National Botanic Gardens in Dublin, and his staff, particularly Donal Synnott, were of great assistance to me in identifying certain grasses and willows, and once again I am grateful to them.

I would also like to thank Ciarán Ó Muirthile and his father, Liam, a member of the Nuacht staff in RTE, for supplying me with a translation of the Irish National Anthem, and the staff of the RTE reference library.

Tom McCaughren, 1989

OTHER ANVIL TITLES BY TOM McCAUGHREN

In Search of the Liberty Tree

The great tide of rebellion sweeps into Ballymena, the
rebels waving green branches and flags ... this is the first
day of liberty. An exciting story of 1798,
seen through the eyes of two boys who became more
than bystanders in the turbulent aftermath.
Illustrated by Terry Myler. 224 pages.

*'A realistic picture of a harrowing time and its effects on the
lives of ordinary people. An excellent read for any history
buff, young or old.'* IRISH TIMES

Ride a Pale Horse

An enthralling and dramatic story which centres on the
fortunes of two boys on opposing sides during a vital
phase of the ill-fated Rebellion of 1798.
Brings vividly to life the armies, the marches,
the councils of war, the camp-followers.
Illustrated by Terry Myler. 144 pages.

'Full of incident and colour, fact and fancy ... a rattling read.'
RTE GUIDE

*'McCaughren conveys graphically the drama and passion
between the supporters and opponents of the United Irishmen
but his real skill is reminding us that beneath the 'abstractions'
known as history there are ordinary lives – including young
lives – whose stories deserve to be heard.'*
ROBERT DUNBAR, IRISH TIMES